A VALENTINE TO CHERISH

JOSIE RIVIERA

INTRODUCTION

To keep up on newly released ebooks, paperbacks, Large Print Paperbacks, audiobooks, as well as exclusive sales, sign up for Josie's Newsletter today.

As a thank you, I'll send you a Free PDF ... The Beauty Of ...

Josie's Newsletter

Did you know that according to a Yale University study, people who read books live longer?

5 STAR READER REVIEWS

"Josie Riviera can write the really emotional stories sometimes. This is one that is that way throughout it all and especially a most beautifully written ending. Get your tissues out as you will need them.

This is such a beautifully written story of a broken heart that is so hard to mend. It's a story of the one person who is willing to make that stand to not hurt the one he loves. He teaches her to love herself as she is and how to let someone into her heart that won't leave.

The small town of Cherish, South Caroline sounds like the perfect small town I want to live in. Our hero found that in himself as well. He travels and doesn't have a real home to come back to. Now here in Cherish he has found his home and it's much more that this quaint town." - **Amazon Reviewer**

"I highly recommend this book not just to read on Valentine's Day like I did, but anytime you need to read about a worthy romance full of everything you want in one.

There are other books in this series so read them all as I am going to." - **Amazon Reviewer**

"Get this book, a cup of your favorite beverage, your tissues and settle into your favorite reading chair and be contented in love that will surround your heart."- **Amazon Reviewer**

"Awesome book!

I love it when the guy is gentle yet strong. Kind and considerate.

The girl has valid issues about her father always leaving, but put God in the mix and there's a HEA.

This is a very enjoyable book to read, and I highly recommend it." - **Amazon Reviewer**

"A very enjoyable read. Christian based, and very sweet. I especially connected to the heroine. Her feelings were also mine...until I met the right one." - **Amazon Reviewer**

This book is dedicated to all my wonderful readers who have supported me every inch of the way.
THANK YOU!

PRAISE AND AWARDS

USA TODAY bestselling author
#1 Bestseller Women's Religious Fiction
#1 Bestseller Contemporary Religious Fiction
#1 Bestseller Inspirational Religious Fiction
Top 100 Christian Short Stories

CHAPTER 1

*S*carlett Evans eyed Joanna, the skinny girl sitting beside her on the wooden park bench. The girl's legs were drawn up to her chest, her limp brown hair parted to the side and pulled into a ponytail. As always, her hair was tangled, as if she'd forgotten about the process of grooming in the middle of the activity.

Scarlett gathered her face into a sunny smile. "Good thing the rain stopped, Joanna."

"Are we going to Dr. Troutman's alpaca farm?" the girl asked.

"He put his farm up for sale last month, remember? There's someone else taking care of the property now, one of his former employees." Scarlett sighed, preferring to forget the slim sandy-haired man who had stolen her heart and then moved away. They'd been in love, or so she'd assumed. Sure, he'd been twice her age and she'd been warned about having a boyfriend twenty years her senior. But he was self-assured and successful, a noteworthy departure from the insecure twenty-something men she had previously dated.

In the end, though, Judson Troutman didn't want to get

married again after losing his first wife, nor did he want to be raising a child in his sixties. At least, that's what he'd divulged the day before his departure when he'd broken their engagement.

Children. A family. That resounding black hole between them.

And, he'd admitted, he'd grown tired of Scarlett's loud, boisterous manner.

Since then, she'd attempted to be quieter, more subdued. Messy and spontaneous? These were fixable traits. Disorganized and overweight? Well, she was working on it.

"I thought you liked alpacas," Joanna said.

"The farm wasn't mine, and it was his choice. I love animals, but truthfully, an entire pasture full of alpacas was more than I could handle by myself. My new job learning how to train service dogs at Canine Helpers is wonderfully rewarding, so at least I'm still working with animals." Scarlett heard the hollow emptiness eddying between her excuses. The alpaca farm would have been perfect and she'd counted on it.

Restlessly, she fiddled with her bright-red shoulder bag.

How foolish to believe that a well-educated veterinarian could fall for a woman like her. A woman who wasn't polished. A woman who was too brash and flamboyant for his refined taste.

Joanna worried the sleeves of her worn pink hoodie. No matter the weather, rain or shine, the hoodie was a staple in her limited wardrobe. "Is he coming back to Cherish?"

"No." Scarlett shook her head as the familiar desolation crept in. All these years she'd dreamed of a man who would truly love her, a man who wanted to share her life.

How had she missed the most important part? She couldn't have a real relationship, because she was afraid to trust and had put up a protective shield.

With good reason. People always left, oftentimes without saying goodbye. She couldn't count on anyone except herself. In the end, she had probably pushed Judson away with her brash manner—an attempt to hide her insecurities.

"Dr. Troutman moved back to his family home in Arizona," she said. "His father fell ill, so he's helping his elderly mother. His parents also own a vet business, and he felt obligated to take it over. That's why he sold his practice here in Cherish."

There it was. More reasons why she had not only lost her fiancé, but also her job as his receptionist when the practice closed.

Quiet enveloped Scarlett and Joanna for a beat, broken by the chirping of a cherry-red cardinal frequenting a bird feeder, designed for the birds as well as the bird watchers. Not far away, a forgotten Christmas ornament hung on a branch of a tall pine tree, the shiny silver bulb catching the sunlight.

Joanna reached for her dog-eared copy of *Fifteen* by Beverly Cleary. At ten years old, the girl was already an incurable romantic. "What about you? Dr. Troutman should've asked you to go with him."

Scarlett hung an arm around Joanna's thin shoulders. "He did. I refused."

He'd asked half-heartedly, but she didn't insert that part. Besides, she was too loyal to Joanna, her Little Sister, to leave her. For Joanna's sake, Scarlett needed to be dependable. The girl had experienced constant disappointment in her young life when her father had abandoned her and her family, and her childhood reminded Scarlett of her own unhappy past.

"Long ago," Scarlett said, "I made a decision to stay rooted in one spot for the rest of my life. I just didn't know where that spot was."

"So you decided on Cherish, South Carolina?" Joanna

gave a horrified burst of laughter. "This town is way too small for me. I want to have an apartment in a big city when I'm eighteen."

"I lived in Chicago my entire childhood and tried to establish roots there as an adult. All I found were flashing neon signs, traffic lights at every corner, and car horns forever honking." Scarlett scooted closer to Joanna. "I landed here after I applied for the job as a receptionist for Dr. Troutman. And now I intend to stay because I love southern towns."

Certainly, people described Cherish as an *if you blink when you pass through, you'll miss it kind of place*, but the picturesque charm appealed to her. As soon as she'd arrived, she'd known she had finally found a hometown.

She reached into the pocket of her bright-yellow raincoat and pulled out a slim chocolate candy bar. With a snap, she offered Joanna half, then glanced at her watch. "Hey, it's almost three o'clock. Wouldn't you rather hang out with your friends on the weekend than with me? It's not too late to text them."

"What friends?" The girl pushed out a dramatic sigh. "You know what I would give to have a real friend right now? Besides you, of course." With those wisely chosen last words, Joanna added an impish chuckle.

"Thanks," Scarlett joked sarcastically before her tone sobered. "Just remember I'm always here for you."

"I know." Pausing, Joanna took a breath. "Although it's just that … as usual, I'm the new girl in town."

"You came to Cherish in September, and it's January."

Before Scarlett could say more, Joanna frowned. Lately, she smiled often, so the frown was unexpected. "I'm uncomfortable when all the students in my class stare at me."

"Then stare back at them."

"I can't." The girl studied her hands. "I'm not friendly and loud like you."

Friendly was a good thing. Loud—not so good. Demure, polite, and ladylike were never traits Scarlett had mastered, but this was a new year. January, the season for fresh beginnings and resolutions.

Soothingly, she tucked a strand of Joanna's brown hair behind her ear. "Remember you're not the new girl anymore, although you're definitely the sweetest."

Scarlett had been matched with Joanna to be her mentor and Big Sister after she'd attended a recruitment asking for volunteers to give of their time. The Big Brothers Big Sisters program was community based, and it focused on low-income families.

Joanna's homelife consisted of her mother, Tania, a slight, ebony-haired woman who incessantly smoked; a scattering of younger siblings; and never enough money to get the family through the month.

"No, you're the sweetest," Joanna said, looking up at Scarlett. "And the prettiest. I wish I had red hair and green eyes and a gigantic smile."

Scarlett grinned, positioning herself so that she and Joanna could hold hands. Here in this park bordered by a hill, they could breathe in trees and fresh air and solitude. The past few months, the park bench had become their place to sit quietly together. Lately, the air smelled of spring—damp soil and grass and new birth.

God promised new beginnings in the normal trappings of daily life. He gave purpose to common situations. Surely, He would help Scarlett not only survive her heartbreak, but be strengthened by enjoying nature and this precious little girl.

Joanna eyed a clump of low-growing pansies, the deep-violet and eye-catching yellow adding vibrancy to the glistening green grass. "Not that I don't appreciate your candy, but I'd love for a boy to give me chocolate for Valentine's Day."

A boy? Stiffly, Scarlett drew back her head. Joanna was certainly growing up fast. She was only in fifth grade, although with today's social media and television programs, kids grew up faster than when Scarlett was young. Still, the idea was disconcerting. Shouldn't Joanna be more interested in roller skating or board games?

Still, she was tempted to say, *Me too*. She kept the contemplation to herself because a candy delivery wasn't coming her way anytime soon. She squeezed Joanna's hand. "But we have each other, right?"

"Right."

That morning had brought rain, a quick storm rattling trees and sweeping across tidy lawns in Scarlett's working-class neighborhood. Now the clouds had parted, and an afternoon sun emerged in a brilliant blue sky, a typical winter day in the Carolinas, where the weather changed from cold to warm within hours. Nearby, dogs barked and teenagers tossed Frisbees to each other.

Scarlett sat against the park bench while Joanna munched her chocolate bar.

"Aren't you going to eat your candy?" Joanna asked between mouthfuls.

"No. You can have mine too." Scarlett handed Joanna her half. She loved candy and crunchy peanut butter ice cream and all kinds of junk food, and deliberated for a half second before giving the candy bar up.

No, no, no. She pushed out a breath. She couldn't count the number of times she'd attempted to diet unsuccessfully. The lead balloon feeling of failure never left, nor its silent counterpart, shame.

Solid looking, people described her. Or, *She has such a pretty face*. Or her favorite, *She's big-boned*. All subtle reminders she should shed thirty pounds.

This time she would lose the weight, she vowed.

She'd heard the cabbage diet worked well, although she'd never liked cabbage.

Tomorrow. She'd begin a new diet tomorrow.

"C'mon, let's head back into town." Scarlett came to her feet and took Joanna's sticky hand in hers. "We can stop for a slice of pizza at Frank's Pizzeria."

At the end of the street, guitar music wafted toward them. People in the park reacted, drifting toward the music, bobbing their heads to the beat of a Christian contemporary song.

"'And we sing, you are our God …'" The tenor male voice resonated through the air.

"Look, Scarlett." Joanna slowed and pointed to a poster mounted to a streetlamp. The poster advertised a Valentine-themed benefit concert sponsored by Musically Yours, the local music store and conservatory. The event would be held outdoors in the park, rain or shine.

The concert was being held to raise money for Cherish Elementary School's music program. Accompanying the poster was a picture of a good-looking man with dark wavy hair, stubble on his chin, and piercing blue eyes.

Joseph Slater, a Christian recording artist, was headlining the event.

"Isn't he handsome?" Joanna had eaten the entire candy bar, evidenced by smears of chocolate on her chin.

"Yes, but he's a musician," Scarlett said.

"Is that good?"

"It means he's busy recording and performing, so hand-some doesn't count because he's unavailable." Scarlett read the poster listing his recent tours and managed a *wow*. Was he ever successful.

"A few months ago, I listened to one of his hits on the Christian station," Scarlett continued. "The DJ went on for five minutes about Joseph Slater because he writes all his own music, as well as songs for various Christian artists. And he was nominated for a Grammy award."

"I knew he was famous." Joanna tented her hands over her eyes and read aloud, "'An international recording phenomenon who recently returned from Australia and is touring the U.S.'" She had a breathless, excited look about her. "We should totally go to the show and meet him. Then you can fall in love again."

At the idea of it—love, dreaming new dreams—a shiver of longing quickened Scarlett's pulse. She believed in the possibility of happily ever after. Just not for her, and certainly not with a touring musician who was here today and gone tomorrow.

"They're selling tickets to the concert at Musically Yours." Joanna tugged on Scarlett's hand. "Don't you know the people who own that music store?"

"Ryan and Dorothy Edwards are dear friends."

"Then you wouldn't want to disappoint your friends, right?"

The joy on Joanna's pale, freckled face had Scarlett fishing for her wallet and hoping she had enough money to cover the ticket prices.

"No disappointments allowed," she declared, counting out a wad of one-dollar bills.

"C'mon." Joanna was off like a rocket, her thin legs moving rapidly toward the music store.

Scarlett couldn't help her smile and quickened her pace. She wanted to attend the concert anyway because she appreciated all kinds of music.

As they rounded the corner, Joanna skidded to a stop.

"That's him! I recognize his picture! Joseph Slater. Playing the guitar."

He sat on a stool in front of Musically Yours, his sharp profile outlined against a sunlit sky. In person, he was even more handsome than his photo. His wavy hair curled at the nape, framing a strong face, straight nose and chiseled jawline. Thoughtfully, he strummed his guitar and sang an inspirational melody to a small enchanted audience. They stood around him and listened intently.

He looked up after he sang his final number, the lyrics about love and peace particularly moving, the deep, rich timbre of his voice striking an unexpected chord in Scarlett's chest.

His clear blue eyes met her gaze.

She sucked in a breath, attempted to wave or applaud, but shelved the idea. Instead, she murmured, "I love that song," to no one in particular. For once, she'd really stopped and listened. The melody was beautiful, and the heartfelt lyrics about trusting God hit her emotionally.

Tears rose in her eyes and she brushed a hand across her lashes.

Silly. She was being silly. Usually, she didn't listen to Christian music, preferring top 40 hits. Besides, she didn't feel comfortable around men who were too good-looking, and this guy lifted drop-dead gorgeous to a whole new level. Attractive guys made her self-conscious about her weight. Besides, in her slick yellow raincoat, she probably resembled a chubby lemon.

She had no idea how many albums Joseph Slater had recorded, but made a mental note to Google him as soon as she returned to her apartment. He'd just topped the number-one spot on her hit list, edging out her favorite rock singer.

"He's staring at you," Joanna whispered.

No. Scarlett was staring at *him* like a gape-mouthed schoolgirl.

He set down his guitar, thanked the audience, and placed the guitar into its case. Smiling an acknowledgement to the cluster of fans, he shrugged on his worn leather jacket, picked up the case, and strode toward her.

Oh my. Now? She was coming face-to-face with him? Now? She must look the size of a house with her wrinkled cotton pants and red boots. And her sweater. She indulged in good cashmere sweaters, although this fitted charcoal-gray one sported a hot fudge sundae graphic on the front. Not exactly a motivation, but the idea of wearing a piece of celery made her inwardly chuckle.

A crisp breeze snapped through the air, and a loose strand of her curly hair fluttered across her forehead. The dampness of the earlier rain had caused her hair to frizz, and she probably looked like she'd been electrified.

As he approached, she felt a jolt of expectation. She and Joanna exchanged glances, and Joanna gave a thumbs up. That is, until he angled past them with a polite smile and entered the music store.

CHAPTER 2

a few minutes later, Scarlett and Joanna greeted Dorothy Edwards inside Musically Yours.

"You're just in time." Dorothy crossed to them and gave Scarlett a teasing, wicked grin. "Joseph Slater is one of Ryan's former classmates. Isn't he all that? And he's a bachelor."

Scarlett paused, at a loss for words. Joseph Slater was well-known for his Christian music, as was Ryan Edwards for his operatic voice.

"I didn't realize Ryan knew him," Scarlett said.

Ryan Edwards, Dorothy's husband, had settled in Cherish when he married Dorothy. They were high school sweethearts, although ten years had passed before they'd met again.

"This way to meet Joseph." Dorothy tugged on the sleeve of Scarlett's raincoat.

Dorothy always looked so polished, her dark hair pinned into a classic chignon, her perfect figure accentuated by a black pencil skirt and burgundy silk blouse.

"There's no need." Scarlett stayed where she was, at the

entry of the music store. She hadn't started her diet yet. Maybe in a year or so.

"Of course there is, because we're all good friends," Dorothy said.

Scarlett twisted her fingers together and eyed the exit. "Joanna and I are here to buy tickets for the Valentine show, but we can come back tomorrow."

"And miss meeting him? You're here now." Ignoring Scarlett's hesitation, Dorothy gaily recited Joseph's numerous awards.

"So your husband went to college with Mr. Slater?" Scarlett asked.

"Mr. Slater?" Dorothy giggled. "That sounds so formal for a casual guy like him. They both received music scholarships to Juilliard. Joseph was only there for a year, though. Then he went on to study worship music in Australia." Dorothy promptly brought Scarlett to the end of a long line. She chuckled at Scarlett's protesting head shake and strolled away with Joanna, showing the girl a stack of musical bracelets—pianos, flutes, and a harp—and encouraging her to pick a favorite.

"I don't play any instrument," Scarlett overheard Joanna saying. "It's hard to choose."

"I think harp lessons will suit you perfectly, so pick a harp bracelet," came Dorothy's reply. "And I know the ideal teacher. Her name is Emmanuelle Thompson and she teaches on Monday evenings. I'll tell Scarlett to bring you back to the store then."

Emmanuelle was Dorothy's sister-in-law who had married Dorothy's brother, Nicholas.

Harp lessons? Scarlett mouthed as Dorothy caught Scarlett's gaze. Dorothy nodded. Obviously, the lessons would be free of charge, and a generous opportunity for Joanna to explore the arts.

Scarlett shifted in line. Mr. Slater sat in a corner behind a desk, autographing CDs.

His leather jacket was slung over a chair. He looked exactly how she imagined a recording artist—the black leather jacket, faded jeans, a white T-shirt that hugged his wide shoulders. The shirt read *Just Have Faith*, and was embellished with a tiny cross.

Have faith? She'd tried that, attempting to lean on her father, praying he'd reciprocate her love for him. She believed in God and attended church. It was just that God had been absent from her life lately.

"Credit your father for doing the best that he can," her mother had encouraged. "Beneath his bad temper, he's a good man."

So Scarlett had tried, while seeking his attention. When she'd been in elementary school her father had propped her up, complimenting her fiery red hair and lively manner. Later in life, when she was an overweight teen, he'd paralyzed her with his indifference.

She blamed her low self-esteem on her upbringing. Beneath her bravado she was almost shy, especially when the man she stood in line to meet was male-model perfect.

Self-consciously, she took a slight step backward when it was her turn.

"Hello, Mr. Slater," she said softly.

There went that handsome-man effect again.

"Hello. Did you purchase one of my CDs that you want me to sign?" Glancing up, he smiled at her guarded retreat, although he didn't remark on it.

"I don't own any. Are they for sale?" Brilliant. Of course they were, which was the main reason he was here. An artist, even an inspirational artist, was probably contracted by his agent to promote, promote, promote.

He nodded toward a stack of CDs placed on a shelf

nearby. "Indeed they are. This CD is a few years old, but the single was nominated for a Grammy."

"Indeed," she echoed blankly. Coupled with her low self-confidence, she was actually starstruck. She began to chuckle at the absurdity of her nervousness. She was a grown woman, not a starry-eyed adolescent.

Surprisingly, his laugh joined hers. "So … did you want to purchase one?" His gaze drifted over her, his astute blue eyes warmly affirming.

"A CD?"

"Yup."

"No. Well, rather, yes." Her hands stilled as she reached inside her shoulder bag. "Unfortunately, I don't have the money. You see, I'm buying two tickets to the Valentine concert, and I only stuck one-dollar bills in my wallet. We had planned on going out for pizza tonight, and then—"

"We? Is that an invitation?"

"No. I mean … Joanna and I." Scarlett could feel the flush of heat on her cheeks. "The little girl—" She was babbling and closed her mouth.

He regarded her for a beat, then reached for a CD on the shelf. He had to duck when he stood. He was tall—probably six feet—and the music store's ceiling sloped at the corners.

"Here." He handed the CD to her. "My treat."

"Your treat for what?"

"For standing in line to meet me. For your preferences. Pizza should always come first, although music and pizza together are perfection. And thanks for the un-invitation."

She laughed.

He grinned, settled in the chair, and uncapped his Sharpie. "What would you like me to write on your CD?"

"Whatever you want," she said. "Best of luck … warm wishes …"

His face lightened with humor. "Do you want me to personalize the message?"

"Sure."

"Should I sign this to you?"

She noted the line lengthening behind her. "Sure. My name is Scarlett. Scarlett Evans."

She peered down while he autographed and recognized her name, although his handwriting was so poor she could hardly decipher it. "That's two *t*'s in Scarlett," she instructed.

"Here you go, two *t*'s Scarlett." He wrote his name and then slid the CD across the table. "My pleasure."

Across the space, their gazes held.

"Thank you." She tucked the CD inside her shoulder bag. "Well, I'm off to buy those tickets."

"I thought you were buying pizza?"

"Oh, right." She was surprised he'd remembered her offhand remark. She shrugged. "Guess not."

"I'll take care of your tickets and leave them with Dorothy. I'm staying at the Cherish Hills Inn for the next few weeks until the concert, so I'll be out and about." He gestured toward the cash register where Joanna sat with Dorothy, swinging her legs on a stool. "Do you need two?"

"Yes, one for me, and one for my—"

"Daughter?"

She cast aside a couple responses. "I don't have any children. I'm Joanna's Big Sister."

The little girl waved gaily at Scarlett and shook her wrist to show off her new harp bracelet.

"Although, wait, please don't buy tickets for us," Scarlett said. "I know the owners and I'll come back to purchase them."

"I know the owners too, and I insist. There's only one catch."

Her head cocked to the side. Was he one of those musicians who assumed no woman could resist him? Would he possibly want to ask her out?

No. She was fairly certain a man of his status wouldn't be interested in a heavy-set small-town woman like her. Unless he was looking for … a fling?

Umm, she wasn't good at flings. And she certainly wasn't about to get hurt again.

"What's the catch?" She tried to keep the wariness from her voice.

He was quiet for several beats. She felt awkward, fingering her shoulder bag.

"Do you sing?" he finally asked. His voice was quiet, deep, velvety.

Taken aback, she chuckled. "Why? Do you need backup singers for your next CD?"

He shook his head. "I'm a soloist."

"Well, then, yes, I sing. That is, if singing in the shower counts?"

"Absolutely." He pressed his hands together. His hands looked strong, his fingertips callused, most likely from endless hours strumming his guitar.

"Should I add the verbs *barely tolerable* to my singing in the shower?" she asked.

"Barely is an adverb."

"Thanks for the English lesson, Mr. Musician." She burst into a wide smile. "What about a tolerable singer?"

"Tolerable is an adjective."

She kept her smile. For a guy who didn't write legibly, he certainly knew his grammar.

Behind her, a man cleared his throat impatiently, which startled her and seemed to visibly annoy Mr. Slater.

"So we've established I'm not a singer," she said.

He rested his hands on the desk and studied her. "You're a good person, being a Big Sister. That's what counts."

She was so disconcerted at the quiet caress in his tone, she blurted, "Although I don't sing well, I love to listen to music."

"Then I'll award you bonus points."

More customers filed into the store. He didn't seem to notice, keeping his gaze fixed on her. It seemed as if he didn't want their conversation to end. Neither did she.

She knew the flush on her cheeks had heightened to a bright pink.

"As long as you love music and promise to attend the concert," he continued, "then the tickets are yours."

No, she thought. He'd done enough, given her a free CD.

"I can't," she said.

"Please, it would mean a lot to me. I pray that my songs will continue to spread God's good word, so I need an audience."

"You're a modern-day writer of hymns, you know that?" She flashed him a smile.

"I used to be." It showed in his eyes, the quick glimpse of frustration before it vanished. He scanned the crowded store, the line behind her. "Not so much anymore."

She didn't know how to answer, eventually murmuring, "I've heard some of the songs you've written and they're amazing."

"Thanks." He signaled to the throat-clearing man to move forward. "I guess some people have been more than patient."

"Guess they are. Sorry," she mumbled to the impatient man as she curved around him.

"Don't forget to come back for your tickets," Joseph Slater said. "I'll leave them at the counter."

She glimpsed Dorothy's attentive expression as she avidly

watched the exchange. Dorothy's interest would soon become an inquisition, then slide into a matchmaking frenzy. She'd been bent on finding Scarlett a man ever since Judson Troutman had left town.

Scarlett couldn't help an inward grin before turning to smile brilliantly at Mr. Slater.

By now, she knew Cherish was different from Chicago, and a person couldn't go far without seeing someone you knew. He'd be in town for several weeks, and she was almost certain to run into him. The thought filled her with unexpected delight.

"Thanks. I won't forget," she said. "Joanna and I will look forward to the concert, Mr. Slater."

"Joseph." He extended his hand, their fingers touching as they shook. A warmth surged through her. She didn't want to let go. His strength was sure and solid.

She sent him an audacious smile and let go of his hand. She began walking away, then called over her shoulder. "Thanks again for your generosity, Joseph."

"That's Joseph with a J," he said.

Beaming, Scarlett expressed her gratitude to Dorothy, and told her friend she'd visit the following day to pick up her tickets. She took Joanna's hand, and the two left the music store and headed for the pizzeria, with Joanna chatting happily about her upcoming harp lesson.

* * *

AN HOUR AFTERWARD, Joseph shrugged on his leather jacket and collected his music as he prepared to leave Musically Yours. The trickle of last-minute customers had cleared out after Dorothy's announcement that the store closed at six o'clock.

"Owning this place is both my business and my passion,"

Dorothy said. She stood behind the counter and clicked her tablet screen while she balanced the money in the cash register. Every inch of space in the store looked inviting, a music lover's haven. Glancing over her shoulder, she added, "But I wouldn't have it any other way."

Joseph looked up. "What did you say?"

"Sorry to interrupt your dreamy-eyed musings." Dorothy's teasing voice roused him from his reflections. "Are you smitten by someone?"

"I'm sure I don't know what you mean." Vaguely, he was aware that Dorothy was watching him. He'd been thinking about Scarlett.

My singing is barely tolerable.

He'd accepted her pleasant jibe at herself with a chuckle. She was quick-witted and good-natured and he'd felt an unexpected pull. He knew it was crazy because of his foot-loose lifestyle. He was never in one city long enough for more than a casual dinner date. He'd nearly forgotten the names of all of them.

The cities. And the women.

Nevertheless, there'd been a spin of warmth, a raw attraction between them. She was enchanting, with lovely sea-green eyes and creamy fair skin. Unconsciously, she'd swayed back and forth while they'd spoken. She didn't seem the type to sit still for long.

Although other fans had been milling impatiently behind her, he'd wanted their conversation to continue, to get to know her a little better. It was unlike him. After finishing the gig in Cherish, he'd head to Raleigh and then New York City. Scarlett obviously lived in Cherish and their paths wouldn't cross again.

He gathered his Sharpies, song list, and business cards and packed them into his duffel bag. His outdoor concert had gone well. Judging by the enthusiastic crowd, promotion for the Valentine event was a success.

He'd arrived in Cherish that morning lethargic and slightly disoriented, jet lagged because of the long flight from Australia. His noise-canceling headphones, combined with the low whirring of the airplane engine, had lulled him into a deep sleep for much of the flight.

In the midst of a dream he couldn't remember, he'd woken at the airport feeling groggy, and the feeling had continued on the train ride from Atlanta to Cherish. After he'd called a taxi at the train station, he'd ridden through the center of town. He'd let down the window and smelled pine trees and greenery and a whiff of spring. A magical morning light enveloped the neighborhood park.

For a moment, he'd been enchanted—until reality and his hectic concert schedule crowded his enchantment.

He shook his head. Admittedly, it would take more hours than he'd anticipated for his body clock to adjust to East Coast time. For the past few years, being on the road brought a weariness he couldn't explain. There was no silence, no peace in his life anymore. He hadn't felt at home anywhere in the world, not even his beloved Australia.

"On the contrary, Joseph, I'm sure you know exactly what I mean." Dorothy went to the door and posted a *We're Closed* sign. "And it's a wonderful idea."

He forced himself to listen to what she was saying. "What is?"

"Dating Scarlett while you're in Cherish." Dorothy walked over to him, pausing to organize some misplaced items on a shelf. "I saw how you looked at her, how you watched her leave the store. You didn't hear the next fan in line speak to you for a solid minute."

"You're right, but there's another word for smitten. It's called jet lag."

Dorothy grinned and handed him a box of CDs. "These are yours."

"Keep them in the store for giveaways. Or better yet, donate them."

"Happily." Chuckling, she arranged them on a display rack. He regarded his photo on the front of the CD, a black and white sketch of him improvising in a recording studio. He'd sat on a stool wearing headphones, playing his guitar, and singing into a microphone.

He hadn't worked in a recording studio for several years, because he had nothing new to record. Sheets of blank manuscript paper crowded his suitcase, waiting like expectant fans.

The last rays of daylight filtered through the shop's front window. How long had he been awake? Australia was sixteen hours ahead of South Carolina time. Did dozing on the plane count?

"In case you're wondering," Dorothy said, "Scarlett and Joanna went to Frank's Pizzeria for dinner. It's a short walk from here."

"She mentioned they were going for pizza." Briefly, Joseph toyed with the idea of joining them. Perhaps after they shared a pizza and chatted for a while, he could walk Scarlett and the little girl home.

"I'm not used to all this walking," he said. "In a big city, I'm either driving on a freeway or in a taxi."

"Living in a small town with sidewalks is better than any fitness center membership."

He chuckled. "Point taken." He made certain to find a gym everyplace he'd visited, knowing exercise kept him fit mentally and physically.

Dorothy went to the counter and shut her tablet. "Cherish is a town of warmth and light."

"You're a poet now?" he teased. "Or am I dreaming about Oscar Wilde because I'm so jet lagged?"

"You're the one who writes beautiful worship music."

"Once upon a time," he said quietly.

"I'd be happy to help you write the lyrics to your next song. That is, if you need any help."

He managed a smile. "I'll keep that in mind."

She went over to a drawer of sheet music and began to file the pieces alphabetically. "Cherish boasts a number of churches too. Ryan and I attend Memorial Street Church," she said. "Pastor Steven and his wife Christina welcome everyone. And Mrs. Marge Addyson, the associate pastor, was speaking just the other day about adding a contemporary worship service to Saturday evening."

He'd wondered where this was leading. Now he knew.

"And this contemporary worship service would be led by … your husband, Ryan?" he asked.

"Unfortunately, he's too busy. He's turned down at least a half-dozen opera roles, and refuses to travel farther than a few hours away from Cherish. Consequently, you're a good first choice." She passed her hand over the music almost lovingly before closing the drawer. "And don't forget, Cherish boasts an equally fine music store and conservatory run by yours truly. Ta-da!"

He grinned and applauded. He couldn't help surveying the tidy store in awe. Every square foot of space had been carefully planned and painstakingly categorized by instrument—piano, harp, guitar, as well as a host of others.

He gazed at a sign prominently hung at the entrance: *Proverbs 19:21: Many are the plans in the mind of a man, but it is the purpose of the Lord that will stand.*

Ryan and Dorothy had built their business on faith, and their diligence and hard work equaled success. Plus, they'd opened a professional music school.

"You and your husband have created a welcoming environment for music lovers of all ages," he said.

"Thanks." Dorothy took an exaggerated bow. "Therefore, you'll get the best of both worlds here. Music and a close-knit, faith-filled town. People in this community are proud to serve the Lord."

"Are you trying to get me to move here?" he half joked.

She grinned. "Maybe."

A track from one of his CDs supplied background music. "My God Is an Awesome God." He'd been inspired to write the song when flying over the ocean, high in a sea of white clouds. For him, every piece of music started with the melody.

"You know my lifestyle," he said. "I don't stay in one place long. Traveling to different locations, hearing my music played at a variety of churches, keeps my muse creative."

He frowned. Did it? Certainly not lately. He hadn't written a new piece in over two years.

He shifted, focused on the stack of unsold CDs.

"Maybe traveling is a season of your life that's over, Joseph," Dorothy said. "Maybe it's time to settle down. Haven't you been on the road at least five years?"

"Ten."

"Is that what you want?"

"It's all I know. Performing music. And writing ..." He focused on the floor, then her. "*Attempting* to write."

She paused, examining his expression. He offered an easygoing smile, hoping she didn't catch the frustration beneath.

"Care to talk about it?" she asked.

"No."

"What if God is withholding what you want to direct you to what you need?"

He didn't answer, scarcely noticing the concern in her

voice. She was echoing a question that continuously nagged at him.

Resting for a week or two in one place between gigs wasn't enough anymore. For a while now, he'd been disheartened when he picked up his pencil to write music that wouldn't come. The door of his first love seemed to have been locked to him. Now it was the door of disappointment.

He believed in being honest. And he was, with everyone but himself. He just couldn't believe God wouldn't let him through that door anymore.

Is that asking too much, God—unlocking my creative muse so that I can compose worship songs again?

An image of Scarlett sparked through his mind. Why did his attention keep drifting to her?

"Do you want me to give you directions to the pizzeria?" Dorothy asked. Before he answered, she grabbed paper and a pen, and jotted down the address. "Scarlett and Joanna should still be there. Besides, you haven't eaten, correct?"

He stuffed the paper into his jacket pocket. "I'll grab something at the inn."

"I know Tom, the innkeeper, and he doesn't do dinner for his patrons. It's a bed and breakfast." Dorothy shut off the music and the lights, a clear sign she was ready to leave. "I'd invite you to our house, but I'm eating leftovers. Ryan is performing in Atlanta tonight, and I don't expect him home until much later. He's taken quite an interest in cooking and I'm encouraging him—mostly because my claim to fame is only pecan pies."

"You can't eat pie every day."

"A sad fact." She grinned. "Although Ryan could and would never gain a pound."

A loving expression came over her face. She and Ryan were so much in love. Joseph had been traveling when they'd married, but he'd spoken to Ryan a number of times and knew the guy was enamored by all things Dorothy.

When Joseph didn't reply, Dorothy asked, "So, you'll be off to Frank's for pizza?"

He hesitated. He shouldn't go. He should rest and listen to what his body was demanding. Get some sleep.

But he was hungry, he rationalized.

And when had weariness ever stopped him before?

CHAPTER 3

$\mathcal{I}$n his beautifully appointed room at the inn, Joseph unpacked and showered.

Although dog-tired, he'd then walked to Frank's Pizzeria. There, he'd been informed by the waitress that Scarlett and her young friend, Joanna, had ordered takeout pizza and left shortly before he'd arrived.

That's what he got for waiting so long.

He ordered a slice of pizza and a soft drink, brought both back to the inn, and then got a decent night's sleep in a luxurious king-sized bed. The linens were top-quality, and the wood plank floor and fireplace exuded homeyness and comfort.

The following morning, Tom, the white-haired innkeeper, prepared a mouth-watering breakfast, setting up tables by a stacked-rock fireplace. After a prayer of thanks, Joseph ate heartily—fresh fruit, homemade corn muffins, a cheese omelet with thick slices of bacon, and hot coffee with heaping teaspoons of sugar.

So now it was noon. Well-rested, overfed, and alert, Joseph zipped up his leather jacket and ventured outdoors.

The weather was brisk and bright, with not so much of a whisper of snow. Ryan had mentioned that Cherish's weather was mild, which proved true on this January day.

After a short walk, Joseph came to Memorial Street Church.

He paused, admiring the picturesque white church, its splendid steeple topped by a cross. He bounded up the church stairs and strode through the open double doors. Kneeling, he clasped his hands and bowed his head.

When would a breakthrough occur so he'd be able to write music again? he asked a silent God. Where was the Lord's blessing on Joseph's life?

True, Joseph had enjoyed the accolades when his songs were well received, the social media explosion of compliments. But he didn't write worship songs for awards and compliments. Did he?

Sometimes he felt like he was fighting a war with the outside world. If he wrote beautiful songs, then people would respect his writing abilities and subsequently, him. And they'd like him. Because it was important to be liked? Wasn't it?

But it was more important to be honorable, to do the right thing for the right reasons. And there was the battle—not with the world and social media. He was fighting a battle within himself.

He shifted on the kneeler. This was his prayer? *This?* Whining and demanding?

He shook his head, closed his eyes, tightened his clasped hands.

None of his failures were God's fault. God wasn't to blame. Any lack of creativity was Joseph's fault. If he got right with God, with himself, then things would fall into place.

As a Christian, he knew this. And if he was more honest,

he'd recognize that his immeasurable pride was in the way of his own blessing. The Lord knew Joseph was far from perfect, yet loved him anyway. Couldn't Joseph do the same, love and respect himself whether or not he was a successful songwriter?

"Through your grace, I will be healed," he prayed.

When he finished and stood, he couldn't determine if his problem had been solved. But he certainly felt more peaceful within himself.

He left the church, retracing his steps, then stopped at a sign mounted on a street corner.

Cherish—one of the most charming towns in the Carolinas.

They'd been spot-on with that description. His breath caught as he crossed to the sun-drenched park and strode around the village green. The town was more peaceful than any he'd seen. Surrounded by budding trees and homespun warmth, Cherish was a special, tranquil place.

He crossed Evergreen Street and discovered a gurgling stream behind an old railway line. Sunbeams glinted off the water's surface, and a scent of moss permeated the air.

"You should see the bluebonnets growing here in the spring," came a familiar voice.

Joseph turned as Ryan Edwards slapped him on the back.

"How are you, my friend?" Ryan asked as the men shook hands. They were the same height. In college, they'd borrowed each other's clothes, which often lay in a dirty heap on their dorm room's floor. None of that mattered then. They were young and carefree.

"Very well," Joseph replied. "You?"

"Couldn't be better." Ryan looked fit and happy, his dark gaze gleaming with contentment. He nodded toward the stream. "When we were teens, Dorothy and I held slingshot contests to see who could snap the most petals off the flowers."

"Who won?"

"Who do you think?' Ryan pulled a hand through his dark-brown hair. "She did."

Joseph chuckled. "Marrying the love of your life obviously agrees with you."

"That's because I married the most beautiful woman in the world."

Tiny specks of snow swirled around them. Here and there, tree branches swayed in a cool breeze. Ryan stuck his hands into his wool jacket and circled toward town. Joseph followed.

"Where are you headed?" Ryan asked.

"Nowhere in particular. Merely exploring the town," Joseph said. "And from what I've experienced in other areas, this weather is almost balmy for winter."

"It's typical South Carolina," Ryan said.

The men fell in step together.

"How was your concert last night?" Joseph asked.

"I sang the role of Gurnemanz in Wagner's *Parsifal* to a sold-out crowd. Are you familiar with the opera?"

"I am. Impressive."

"Thanks. I'm still able to perform in big cities like Atlanta, come home to my lovely wife at the end of the day, and join her at church services on Sunday."

"*Therefore, you'll get the best of both your worlds here,*" Dorothy had said, voicing her not-so-subtle opinion. "*Music, and a close-knit, faith-filled town.*"

"Is your life as easy as all that?" Joseph asked.

"No one said it was easy," Ryan said. "But I'm discovering a joy I once believed was elusive."

"Traveling is hard, though?"

"Yes. Although it's worth it when you're doing something you love." Ryan blew out a breath. "Admittedly, Atlanta is a long drive and I didn't arrive home until well after midnight.

Fortunately, Dorothy insisted on hiring an Uber for me, so I slept in the car all the way back."

When they reached the middle of town, Ryan gestured to a restaurant across the street from them. "Hey, if you haven't eaten lunch yet, I highly recommend The Garden Terrace."

Joseph patted his stomach. "I'm still full from breakfast, although I'd love a glass of something cold."

"We're in the south, so order sweet iced tea and a slice of sugar-free lemon cake. You'll never taste anything better." Ryan glanced at his watch. "I'd join you, but I promised Dorothy I'd take over at the music store this afternoon so she can have a break. We'll catch up later, okay?"

Joseph could think of nothing more inviting than finding a discreet corner in the restaurant where he could unwind. "Sounds good. Although my sweet tooth will demand regular lemon cake, not sugar free."

"The restaurant serves both. Enjoy." With a quick *later,* Ryan spun toward the music store.

The wooden door to the restaurant creaked as Joseph opened it. He slid into a booth at the rear and glanced around. Dimly lit, the place had a sense of timelessness, boasting thick wooden beams on the ceiling and deer antlers mounted on the walls. An appetizing array of grilled meats and homemade barbecue wafted in the mesquite-filled air.

Intending to peruse a menu for a light appetizer to go along with the lemon cake and iced tea, he noticed Scarlett sitting at a booth near the front. She dined with an older man who faced her. Although her back was to Joseph, he'd recognize her anywhere. Her red hair fell in curls over her shoulders. Deep in conversation, she bobbed back and forth. Her shoulder bag was set beside her.

Joseph studied the man, who resembled Scarlett in so many ways, he assumed he was her father. The man had the same strong facial features and wisps of red hair as Scarlett, although he was as thin as a popsicle stick, and his eyes, even from a distance, were watery and bloodshot.

Joseph ordered a sweet iced tea, then thanked the young waitress with spiked black hair as she set the glass in front of him. He grabbed three sugar packets to doctor up his tea to a sugar max.

"It's already sweet," the waitress reminded him.

"Not sweet enough."

She shrugged. "Anything else? We're known for our sugar-free lemon cake."

"So I've heard. I was going to order an appetizer too, but tea is good for now." He shut the menu and handed it to her. He'd changed his mind, preferring to watch Scarlett and her father. "Maybe next time."

"Thanks." She smiled and left the bill on the table.

He took in every detail of the bustling restaurant and soaked in the ambiance—the older couple to his left, sitting side by side, silently concentrating on their meals. The collapse of giggles from two teenage girls.

Joseph took out a notebook and pen he always carried in his pocket and swung his gaze toward Scarlett's table. As a songwriter, he liked to watch people and considered himself intuitive for analyzing what went on with them.

He waited for lyrics to come. Closed his eyes. Waited some more. Nothing flowed. Pinching his lips together, he stuffed the notebook back into his pocket.

As he glanced up, he noticed that the conversation at Scarlett's table had quieted.

She pushed her plate full of salad to the side. Shaking her head, she toyed with a straw in her tall glass of lemonade.

The older man's face reddened. Unexpectedly, he slapped his hand on the table.

Scarlett jumped and the patrons around them paused to stare, then averted their gazes.

Immediately, Joseph sensed the constraint between father and daughter. Although Scarlett froze in place, she attempted conversation again. In response, the man's gaze wandered, and he answered in monosyllables.

On his feet five minutes later, the older man briefly clenched his fingers, followed by words that Joseph couldn't make out.

Another beat, and Scarlett and her father left the restaurant. Outside, the man kept his hands in his pockets while she gave him a quick, awkward hug. As the two departed, they walked in opposite directions. He climbed into a big rig parked to the side.

On impulse, Joseph bolted up, threw money on the table for his iced tea plus a tip, and rushed through the exit.

"Scarlett!" he hailed as he sprinted toward her.

She paused, then whirled. "Mr. Slater?"

"Joseph with a J, remember?"

"Of course." Her voice was strained. She lifted her chin, a sheen of tears in her glorious green eyes. She wore a pink paisley scarf that complemented her peaches-and-cream complexion. Her wool coat was forest-green with a high shawl collar. A navy sweater peeked from beneath, offering a glimpse of a sequin-embossed butterfly. He liked her colorful style and openly admired her shapely figure.

"Umm." She pulled at the front of her coat. "Why are you staring at me?"

Whoops. He swung his gaze to the sidewalk, although it drifted appreciatively back to her face. "I noticed you and that man in the restaurant."

Who was he? Joseph wanted to ask, but stopped himself. He waited to see if she would explain.

She didn't.

"Was he your father?" he couldn't help asking.

"Yes."

"And?"

Ignoring the question entirely, she hooked her shoulder bag on her arm and looked around the street.

Alrighty then.

"A coincidence we were both leaving at the same time," he said into the silence. "I was wondering if you could recommend …" He thought fast, pulling a hand through his hair. "Recommend a good place for a haircut. I wasn't able to schedule a trim before I left Australia."

"Cherish Styles and Clips is a short walk from here. They offer a full-service hair salon for both men and women, and I know the owner, Phyllis. I helped her move into her new place a few months ago." Scarlett pointed to an intersection diagonally from them. "Take a left on that corner, then a right. A couple more blocks and you're there."

"Can you walk with me? I've been known to get lost on a one-way dead-end street."

Not at all true, but he couldn't make himself be concerned with details. He wanted to spend time with her. His conscience tapped him on the shoulder. He'd just seen her the day before, remember?

He stiffened. And? Couldn't he see a woman twice in two days? Nevertheless, his excuse to spend time with her was anything but brilliant. A haircut. Really? So much for being a well-known lyricist. No wonder he couldn't write a noteworthy song anymore.

"Sure," she agreed. "I'll walk with you."

He could scarcely take his eyes off her as she guided him to the corner. They kept their pace slow as she pointed out local landmarks, then gestured to the streetlamps.

"Soon, the town will hang baskets of yellow and red petunias all along the main streets," she said. "On a sunny afternoon in May, the colors are amazing."

He wouldn't be here in May. For the first time, he understood what that meant and felt a twinge of regret. He'd seen streetlamps and flowers before, but with Scarlett, everything took on a fresh perspective. The whisper of snow, the comfortable strolling, the rays of a wintry sun, felt different.

"Cherish is even prettier than a postcard," he said.

They lingered to admire a shop window featuring a male and female mannequin dressed in red, standing in front of a white background. *Follow Your Heart*, the exhibit stated in bold red letters, with a string of rosy Valentine hearts taped to the window.

"Cherish celebrates every holiday," Scarlett said. "Some are more important than others." A softness came over her expression, making her look younger and somehow vulnerable.

"Where does Valentine's Day rank in holiday importance?"

"For the town?"

"For you."

"Near the top," she said quietly. A gust of wind ruffled her shiny hair. He wanted to stroke his hands through her curls. He wanted to hold her, right here in the middle of this appealing town. He wanted—

No. What was he thinking?

He cleared his throat. "Anything else?"

"Anything else about what? The town?"

"About you." He knew the difference between talking and listening, so he steered the conversation toward her. He wanted to listen. "For example, tell me about your Little Sister. You mentioned her name was Joanna."

"Where do I start?"

"How about at the beginning?"

"Well, I enrolled at the Big Brothers Big Sisters organization, then went through an extensive interview process to become a mentor."

"What are the requirements?" he asked.

"Applicants need to be eighteen years old. At the age of thirty, I was welcomed."

He laughed. "I'm thirty-five."

"You'd be approved too. You seem stable and would probably be a positive role model."

He couldn't contain his grin. "Probably?"

"Dorothy and Ryan speak highly of you, so I'll amend that probably to a definitely." She shared his grin. "The goal of mentoring is faith, and for the child to have confidence in you. They need to know you won't let them down."

Faith again.

"A mentor doesn't need to be rich or famous," she added, throwing him a meaningful look.

He was certainly not wealthy, as he donated half of the proceeds from his CD sales to charities. Famous? He shook his head. Hardly, although Scarlett might refute him.

Farther along the sidewalk, she stopped to study the ice-cream flavors on a sign posted outside Whitney's Ice Cream. Wistfully, she sighed and pointed to peanut butter crunch ice cream, describing it as creamy, decadent, and, well, crunchy.

"The crunch is the rice cereal," she explained. "And it's delicious."

The outdoor dining space beside the restaurant hosted an array of tangerine-colored, wrought-iron tables.

"Want to buy a cone?" Joseph stepped forward, examining the long list of flavors. "Do they carry candy?"

He could get a haircut anytime, he rationalized.

"Candy? Ice cream? You're joking, right?" With her corkscrew curls bouncing around her shoulders and a mischievous gleam in her eyes, Scarlett presented a delightful picture. "I'm staying far away from peanut butter crunch ice cream. It's one of my red-light foods."

"Which means?"

"If I have it around, I'll eat the entire container."

He was torn between drawing her closer for a kiss, or the similarly pleasant notion of feasting his gaze on her. For now, he decided to gaze at her.

"You'll need to go down the street to Charlie's Chocolatiers for your candy," she said. "Just don't ask me to taste anything because I'm on my ten-thousandth diet." A strand of hair fell across her eyes. She didn't push it away. "Which started today."

"Why?"

"Really?" She gave a small smile. "Look at me."

She was beautiful and full of life, and his heart skipped several beats as he studied her from head to foot.

"You don't need to diet. You look great."

"You've been traveling too long," she said. "Particularly in Western culture, women are encouraged to be as skinny as possible."

"I don't agree." He couldn't get his compliments out fast enough. "Truly, you're absolutely lovely."

A rosy flush crept across her high cheekbones, and her chin trembled.

"Hardly," she said, so quietly, he barely heard her.

So there were definite chinks in the armor beneath her smile.

And he wanted to get past the armor.

Nope, don't go there. No long-distance romances. He was leaving Cherish in a few weeks. Moreover, he'd closed himself off from emotional attachments and his barricade was firm. Two disastrous relationships in two different cities had been enough.

But the way Scarlett had brightened when he'd asked about Joanna, her cupid-shaped mouth and her eyes shining like polished emeralds, chiseled away at his barricade's unguarded cracks.

They resumed their walk.

"You were asking me about the Big Brothers Big Sisters program," Scarlett said. "Still interested?"

He gazed at her. "More than ever."

"The organization matched Joanna and me up. She comes from a single-parent home and faces difficult obstacles. This particular transition has been tough. The poor kid moved five times in three years, and she hasn't seen her father in ages." Scarlett took a handkerchief from her shoulder bag and dabbed at her eyes. "As she matures, it's my job to steer her away from risky behaviors."

"You fix things for her. You protect her. Bravo."

"As best I can, although that's not my role." Reaching into her bag again, she lifted out a small album with photos of Joanna—at the library, at the park, at the movies. Through the progression of time, Joanna's transformation from a sullen girl to a young lady bearing a proud posture was remarkable. In the last photo, dressed in a pink polka-dotted sweater dress, Joanna smiled broadly and gave a thumbs-up. She stood outside Memorial Street Church with an older woman and looked directly into the camera.

He nodded approvingly. "Who's the lady with the bright-red rouge?"

"Mrs. Marge Addyson, the associate pastor. A lovely woman, widowed, and she views everything in a Christian, down-home way. If you get a chance to meet her, you'll know what I mean. She's wonderful to Joanna, and is a mentor too."

"Every minute I'm in Cherish, I find more people to admire. You all follow the Lord's example of giving. Dorothy, Ryan, Mrs. Addyson, you …"

"We try our best. I'm here for Joanna to lean on and to share opportunities," Scarlett said. "Such as the Valentine tickets you bought for us, and the harp lessons Dorothy graciously offered."

"I bet you're a remarkable influence."

"I hope so." She indicated the harp bracelet on her wrist. "Joanna insisted that she and I wear matching bracelets, although I'm no harpist. It was a surprise and so considerate, along with Dorothy's big-heartedness, of course." Scarlett puffed a deep breath. "Soon Joanna will enter middle school. She'll face difficult choices—drugs, alcohol, peer pressure. I'll be there to steer her on a positive, Godly path."

"Joanna got lucky when her family moved to Cherish."

"Millions of kids need an adult role model. And I'm the lucky one. Joanna is smart and funny and has a heart of gold. I'm in and fully committed."

"How long is the program?"

"The organization asks mentors for a yearly commitment, which is no problem." Scarlett's entire face lit up. "It's understandable, because it takes time for a child to build up trust."

"Are you involved in any other worthy causes?" In the spirit of their comfortable rapport, he took her hand as they rounded the last corner to the hair salon.

She didn't pull away.

"Well, I love animals, although that's not really a cause. It's more like my passion. I was the receptionist at a veterinarian practice in town before it shut down." Her expression closed, briefly unreadable. "Currently, I'm learning how to train service dogs at Canine Helpers. It's part-time, Monday through Friday, and Thursday I work a half day."

"Service dogs for …"

"Any person with a disability who can benefit from the service. These dogs help disabled people lead a more independent life."

"Define disability."

"Any physical or mental impairment that limits a person."

"Fascinating." He squeezed her hand, and they continued in silence. It seemed like they could have a conversation without ever having to say anything. That was how in tune he felt with her. "I'd like to hear more about it."

A tap on the shoulder again from his annoying conscience.

In tune with her? How? You've only known her a short time.

"Anytime," Scarlett said. "Oh, and did you know dogs are the only species recognized as service animals?"

"Not horses?"

"Good question." Approvingly, she nodded. "No, not horses. Although miniature horses are regulated and sometimes used."

He smiled as they reached the entrance to Cherish Style and Clips. Purple pansies accented the shop's window boxes. "Any other worthy causes you'd like to share with me, Scarlett?"

"I like to call them passions, remember?"

"Passions, then. Even better." They were still holding hands. Beneath his fingertips, her skin was smooth and delicate.

"Cooking is my specialty," she said. "No shock there, I'm sure." Another deprecating laugh. She did that often, and there was no need. Didn't she realize how perfect she was?

"Any special recipe?" he asked.

"I've prepared a tasty meatloaf and mashed potatoes recipe my friend, Cathie, gave me. She works with me at Canine Helpers. The meatloaf is comfort-food delicious, and uses a homemade barbecue sauce with brown sugar and spicy brown mustard and tomato sauce."

"I'd like to try that sometime." Yes, dinner at her place sounded just the thing.

He knew he was staring at her mouth, and forced himself to look away.

Overhead, the sun was high. An abrupt gust of cold wind reminded that spring was still a couple months away. Notwithstanding, a young couple strolled past arm and arm, swinging a picnic basket.

Probably on route to the park, Joseph surmised. Already, he was getting to know the layout of the town.

Scarlett's gaze flicked to the hair salon, then back to him. "Are you asking me to cook dinner for you?"

"Is that too bold?" He took a step closer. He couldn't help himself. Everything about her intrigued him.

"No. I love to cook."

Lightly, his fingers grazed her cheekbone. "And I won't need dessert," he said softly. "You're sweet enough."

She retreated a step and pulled her hand from his. "This isn't a good idea."

"What? Cooking meatloaf?"

"This." She moistened her lips. "Us."

"Why?"

"Because you're in Cherish for a few short weeks. And I'm here …"

"For the long haul." He finished her sentence. His gaze focused on her mouth again. Without thinking, he bent down and his lips brushed against hers. She tasted like fresh-squeezed lemonade—refreshingly tart, yet sweet.

She didn't stir, although she inhaled slightly. He hoped it was a sigh of pleasure.

"So we can date while I'm in Cherish," he murmured against her lips.

"You are so not listening." She shifted another step back. "You're a world traveler who has undoubtedly dated scores of women and then gone on to the next big city. I will not be one of those women." She pivoted, then seemed to change her mind as she curved back to him. "Thank you for the tickets, though."

He was still reeling from her refusal. He covered his disappointment with the lazy grin he'd adapted over the years. "You're welcome, Scarlett. Enjoy the concert. Thanks for showing me the way to my first haircut in weeks."

"Anytime. And say hi to Phyllis." A hint of a smile crossed her face. "Don't let her talk you into dyeing your hair purple or anything like that."

His gaze slid meaningfully to her hair. "I won't, as long as you stay a redhead."

"You never know." Her smile widened. "I always liked green."

"In your hair?"

"A few green highlights will complement the red. And the color green symbolizes nature."

"And red symbolizes a fiery personality."

"But not everybody can pull off both colors at once."

"You can, because you're amazing." He grinned, admiring her spirit, and said goodbye.

Goodbye for now, he amended.

As he entered the busy hair salon and took a seat, he was informed that Phyllis had the day off. Furthermore, as a walk-in customer, he would need to wait at least thirty minutes before a hairdresser could fit him in.

"No worries," he replied. The half hour gave him the opportunity to think about Scarlett. Her laughter, her optimism, her obvious passion about the things she cared about were utterly appealing. And they all revolved around three themes.

Faith. Service to others. Home.

Faith. He got that. He prayed that he could harness her faith, as his was elusive lately, and he was fast becoming a sorry excuse for a worship songwriter. How could he feel good about himself when he wanted God's guidance, but wasn't willing to make any sacrifices that went along with it?

Lately, his songwriting attempts had been half-hearted, and many times he'd given up before he began.

Service to others. Sorely lacking on that front too, he reflected. He'd visit the Big Brothers Big Sisters organization in Cherish to see if he could mentor in some way while he was here.

Home. For him, that was wherever he happened to be. He was on a never-ending trek to see the world.

With Scarlett, however, things were different. She was an obvious homebody.

Usually, he'd be looking right about now for the fastest way out of town if he had so much of an inkling that he was attracted to a woman like her.

But he couldn't, because he couldn't deny her desirability. Everything about her intrigued him. However, his reluctance to settle down in one place weighed equally as strong.

CHAPTER 4

*T*he next morning, Scarlett awoke to the incessant ringing of her cell phone. Blinking in bewilderment, she checked the time and glanced at the caller ID.

"Hi, Dorothy," she answered groggily.

"I didn't wake you, did I?" came Dorothy's reply.

Sluggishly, Scarlett opened her eyes to a peek of morning sun filtering through her bedroom's sheer white draperies.

"Nope. I'm always awake by seven a.m."

"Joseph came by our house last night with an idea," Dorothy said. "In fact, he and Ryan talked about it for hours. We wanted to run it by you."

"What is it?"

"Joseph wants a kids chorus from the Big Brothers Big Sisters organization to sing back-up for two of his songs at the Valentine concert, and he's hoping you'll help."

Well, whoa. Scarlett placed the phone in her lap and regarded her freckled hands, her clenched fingers. He hadn't mentioned anything of the sort the day before. And why was her stomach doing a somersault at the thought of seeing him again?

She had to think, reviewing the facts she'd gathered about him. She shouldn't be nervous. He'd been kind and pleasant the entire time they'd been together. And he was extraordinarily well-liked, evidenced by the excitement at the music store when she'd waited in line. That radio DJ had carried on and on about him too. And her dear friends, Ryan and Dorothy, spoke well of him.

So what was Joseph's motive? More advertising?

Unlikely. She couldn't imagine he'd seek more publicity, especially for a benefit concert. He seemed like he wanted to spread the word of the Gospel, a genuinely good Christian man.

And a handsome one at that.

Her heart fluttered at the image of his chiseled features and sparkling blue eyes. Did he know how good-looking he was? Did he know those good looks were intensified by his quiet charm, his apparent unawareness of his appeal?

Scarlett brought the phone to her ear. "What about my ticket? And Joanna's?"

"Joseph said to donate them. Perhaps a couple people from Canine Helpers might want to go."

Scarlett's mind scrambled for another excuse. "But Joseph is a professional solo artist. He wouldn't want a kids' chorus accompanying him."

"He's requesting something different. His pieces are beautiful and timely and the audience can sing along too," Dorothy said. "Did you know his songs are sung all over the world?"

"Yes. I checked his biography on the internet last night." Scarlett's cheeks warmed at her admission. The previous evening, she'd spent hours indulging her interest in him while she watched him sing and perform on YouTube. No matter how many times she'd scolded herself not to, she'd been too enthralled by his concerts to do anything except watch in admiration. He'd also been interviewed by a famous Christian pastor in Australia, and had responded to the pastor's questions with effortless grace. The clip had received numerous hits on YouTube.

"His biography stated that he hasn't written a new single in a while," Scarlett noted.

"He said he's been inspired to write a couple new songs. We'll record at least one at the concert, and it will get first-hand coverage by the local TV and radio stations."

"Record it where?"

"Ryan installed a recording studio in the conservatory's rehearsal room, complete with a computer, microphones, headphones, studio monitors—you name it. Now when he's recording music for opera auditions, he won't need to leave home."

"Your expansion efforts are nothing short of remarkable."

"Thanks. The Lord has truly blessed us." Dorothy hesitated. "So you will help us, won't you?"

Hauling herself up to a sitting position, Scarlett fluffed the pillows behind her and then collapsed against them. With more curiosity than enthusiasm, she asked, "How?"

"Well, you're involved in Big Brothers Big Sisters. Joseph suggested you be in charge of enlisting five kids to sing with him."

"I don't sing, so I'm no expert. Will I need to audition the children?"

"Of course not. He doesn't want perfection. And I assume you'll include Joanna because she'll love it."

Scarlett took a sip from the water bottle on her night-stand. Dorothy was right, of course. The kids would be thrilled. Joanna would be thrilled. The community would be thrilled.

But what about Scarlett? Her heartbeat accelerated at just

the thought of seeing Joseph again, working side by side with him.

Be rational, she told herself. This wasn't about her.

Okay.

Then she could admit she was ridiculously nervous about the entire undertaking. Joseph made her feel like a girl with her first crush, and she couldn't tamp down her attraction to him.

"Scarlett?" Dorothy asked. "Are you still there?"

"Of course." Scarlett studied the beams of sunlight creeping across her beige carpet.

"Without your assistance, his idea might not fly," Dorothy said. "He said you'll need to be at every rehearsal."

"Okay."

"What does that mean? Is that all you can say?"

Scarlett shoved a hand through her hair. "What do you want me to say? Somehow, I think this was all decided without me."

Dorothy laughed. "Just say *yes* with an exclamation point. What's stopping you?"

Joseph, she thought. Being close to Joseph.

But how could she share these reservations with Dorothy, or the fact that Scarlett had been thinking of little else but him since they'd walked to the hair salon the day before?

"Nothing's stopping me," she replied, tempering her voice. She didn't want to sound too enthusiastic. She didn't want Dorothy's matchmaking antenna to go up any higher than it already had.

"Consequently, you're good with this then, right?" Dorothy pressed. "We all assumed you would jump at the chance."

Aha. "Really? You all assumed?"

"Well, yes."

"Even Joseph?"

46

"It was his idea. He said you can be his assistant director."

Scarlett gave an exasperated shake of her head. She had informed him she didn't want to get personal while he was in Cherish. Apparently, he followed his own agenda.

Once more, she set the phone in her lap. With a sigh, she looked around the empty bedroom. So why would he assume she'd jump at the chance?

Reason one: Because he suspected she was already interested in him. She hoped her feelings weren't that obvious.

Reason two: He knew she'd never disappoint Joanna. A practical explanation.

Her heart, however, chose a different reason. Perhaps *he* wanted to spend time with *her*, thus using her involvement with Big Brothers Big Sisters as an excuse.

She couldn't contain her smile. She couldn't contain her hope, either. That is, until she quickly shoved aside that notion.

She refused to live in a fantasy world. He was a famous musician who had visited more countries than she could count on two hands. She was an overweight woman living in a small town. A woman whose fiancé had left her flat. A woman who, beneath her bright outward appearance, was self-doubting.

"You can't control your emotions," she'd once heard a pastor say, "but you can control your focus." And her focus should be about others, not herself.

"Scarlett? Where did you go now?" Dorothy asked through the muffled phone receiver.

"I'm here." Quickly, Scarlett pushed out a breath and drew the phone to her ear. "And I'd love to help."

"Great. I assume you'll stop at Big Brothers after work? I'll drop Joseph's music off there, so the kids can take a peek."

"As soon as my shift at the service-dog facility is over at

three o'clock," Scarlett replied. "And Dorothy, thank you. The idea sounds beneficial for the entire community."

"Yay! I agree."

The happiness and relief in her friend's voice almost reduced Scarlett to tears.

Sternly, she reminded herself she hadn't agreed because she'd have the opportunity to work with Joseph. She'd agreed because it was an amazing break for the children. Plus, not only would the concert provide delightful worship music for the town, but it also supported things that mattered—money for the elementary school's music program, and a one-of-a-kind experience.

A few minutes later, Scarlett sat at her chrome kitchen table eating a healthy breakfast—fat-free Greek yogurt, a banana, and black coffee. Today was another day of her diet, and she felt excited and motivated. As she sipped her coffee, she went about convincing herself that this new undertaking with Joseph could also be healthy for her in a personal way.

Often in the past, she'd run away from anything that scared her.

In this case, working with a man who made her heart go into overdrive would be good therapy. This time, she wouldn't avoid the situation. She'd have to get over the fact that this tall, handsome musician brought up unresolved sadness from her childhood just by standing next to her.

These were feelings she preferred to keep under a protective bubble, but she wouldn't disappoint her friends and Joanna for anything in the world.

Would she?

Drop by drop, she felt her self-assurance draining away and swallowed hard.

Wasn't this how difficult things worked? A person faced challenges directly in order to move on.

She leaned back in her chair, placed her hands behind her

head, and glanced out the window. Already, the sky promised a gloriously sunny day.

She relaxed her muscles and stood. Her steps to her bedroom were swift and purposeful.

* * *

AT THREE THIRTY in the afternoon, Scarlett arrived at the brick building on Main Street that housed Big Brothers Big Sisters. She'd successfully finished her work at the service-dog facility, training a German Shepherd to switch on the lights inside a home for a man suffering from PTSD. The man, Mark, had recently returned from combat duty over-seas and was feeling wary about his safety. The dog gave Mark a sense of security and also served as a physical barrier between him and the outside environment. Plus, the shep-herd forced Mark to exercise—going outdoors to walk the dog. A win-win on all counts.

Pausing at the entrance to Big Brothers with her hand on the brass door handle, Scarlett cleared her thoughts and swept inside.

Isaac Albertson, the director, was in his office. He stood with his back to her, studying the large bulletin board that listed the week's activities for the children and their mentors. He stepped out of his office to greet her with an enthusiastic hand slap.

"Are you here to see Joanna and your new chorus?" He reached for a leather briefcase and handed it to her. "Dorothy dropped this off for you." He grinned, and his silver-white mustache lifted. His balding head shone in the overhead fluorescent lights.

"Thanks. You heard about the children's chorus, then?" Scarlett unzipped the briefcase and peered inside. Five copies of Joseph Slater's sheet music entitled, "And We Sing,

You Are Our God" were neatly filed, the lyrics clearly typed.

"Dorothy briefed me, and the idea is excellent," Isaac said. "I asked all the elementary kids. Five are ready and willing. One is Joanna, and there are two other girls and two boys. I've checked with their parents, and permission slips are all signed."

"Wow, you are efficient."

"Shh." He pressed a finger to his lips. "Don't let word get out. Someone at the state level may want to cut my hours."

Scarlett grinned and couldn't help thinking that without Isaac's tireless work and enthusiasm, the organization in their little town would never have grown to the proportions it had. This brick building was just one small haven in a big, dangerous world, but it meant so much to these precious children.

Isaac followed her to a large gymnasium full of noise and confusion and laughter. Some children read books aloud with their mentors, others played board games, while a group of middle-school boys shot baskets.

"Here's your charges." Isaac gestured to a group of children sitting at one table. "Two are third-grade girls, and the other two are fourth-grade boys."

"And me," Joanna reminded as she stood. "I'm in fifth grade."

Scarlett grinned at the youngsters as they gathered around her.

"You're a great bunch," she said. "Can anyone sing?"

They all raised their hands. That is, every child except one of the fourth-grade boys. With a defeated slump of his shoulders, he said, "I don't want to be in the concert after all."

"Why not?" she asked.

"My older brother will call me a sissy." He jutted out his chin. "Besides, I can't sing."

"Do you want to be in the concert?"

He shuffled his feet and looked down. "Yes," he mumbled.

"Remember, different people are good at different things. And I know if you work hard, you'll do great." She offered her most encouraging smile. "It will be fun, and I promise lots of great men are artists."

"Promise?"

"Promise. So will you sing with the other children?"

He peered up at her through a curtain of black bangs and nodded.

Isaac led the children into a rousing rendition of "Row, Row, Row Your Boat," then handed out the music to Joseph's song and read through the lyrics with them. When they finished, Scarlett applauded and shouted, "Bravo!"

The dark-haired fourth-grade boy peered up at her. "I'm Russell."

"I'm Scarlett."

He held a half-eaten chocolate cupcake in his hand and offered it to her.

She scooped him up. "Thank you, but I'm on a—" She was cut short when the boy threw his arms around her neck and gave her a chocolate-frosting-laden kiss.

"I really want to be in the concert," he whispered.

"Hurray!" She took a bite of his cupcake and smiled while her heart melted. What would she do without these kids? They'd enriched her life in more ways than she'd ever imagined.

After using the restroom, the children retrieved their coats, then Scarlett and Isaac herded them out of the building. They had so much energy, passersby chuckled at their boisterousness. They walked two blocks and took a right down Evergreen Street to Musically Yours. Isaac marched the children in single file through the music store, reminding them to be on their best behavior. As always, the store looked bright and hospitable, welcoming musicians and music lovers alike.

Emmanuelle Thompson, a lovely woman with silky blond hair, huge blue eyes, and a face that seemed carved out of bone china, smiled a greeting at Scarlett while assisting a customer. Scarlett paused to stop and say hello.

Emmanuelle was Dorothy's sister-in-law, having married Dorothy's brother Nicholas, the deputy in town.

"No children yet," Emmanuelle had once said to Scarlett with a laugh. "Nicholas and I are content with our dog, Molly Belle. Believe me, she keeps us extremely busy."

Emmanuelle had once been principal harpist in a prestigious orchestra. Nowadays, she taught harp lessons, performed locally, and worked in Musically Yours.

When Scarlett reached the large rehearsal room at the back of the store, she stopped to talk with Ryan, who was setting up a row of five chairs. While they chatted, the children bounded for the chairs like a shot.

After Isaac seated everyone, he took the opportunity to leave, explaining he needed to stop back at Big Brothers Big Sisters. He'd been asked to expand the mentoring program to a neighboring county, was meeting with a group of interested volunteers, and was sorry he couldn't stay. He didn't look the least bit sorry, Scarlett thought with an inner smile. Isaac was dedicated to the organization, but preferred his quiet office rather than a group of rambunctious children.

Dorothy sat at the upright piano, her fingers poised on the keys, ready to accompany the songs in a supporting role for the rehearsals. Joseph had claimed one of the two empty stools beside her. Despite Dorothy's pointed stares, he ignored her. He plucked the strings of his guitar with his long fingers, sang softly, and then hastily scribbled notes on a sheet of manuscript paper. The melody was lovely and one that Scarlett didn't recognize.

Even in this concentrated pose, with his brow furrowed in utter concentration and his full lips pressed together, she needed to assure herself that he was real. This handsome, famous man, wearing worn jeans and a long-sleeved navy T-shirt, was rehearsing for a concert in a town so small, it had only one elementary school.

He didn't belong here. He belonged on a concert stage performing for thousands of avid fans, as he'd performed at the Grammy awards on national television.

No, she corrected herself. He looked completely comfortable and in his element—singing in an environment with other professional musicians.

She was the one who didn't belong. She didn't know anything about music. She only knew about children and animals, cooking and volunteer work. She couldn't even sing on pitch in the shower.

She glanced down at her clothing, hastily picking the dog hairs off the sleeves of her green coat. Beneath the coat, she'd worn a color-block sweater in a flashy pink and purple, fitted blue jeans that were admittedly a tad too tight, and gray leather ankle boots. Any stylish effect was ruined by her unkempt hair piled in a side bun, and the chocolate frosting stain on the sleeve of her coat. The makeup she'd applied that morning had faded, and she hadn't had time to reapply lipstick.

Keeping her position in the doorway and feeling utterly self-conscious, she watched Ryan walk away and grab a bottled water from a cooler. While her insecurities tumbled in her mind and she considered retreating, she stole another surreptitious glance at Joseph.

She had vowed not to run from the situation, she reminded herself. She would be here for the rehearsals leading up to the Valentine concert. She was a Big Sister, a mentor. A woman Joanna could depend on. Without Scarlett's friendship, Joanna's precarious security and self-worth issues could be turned inside out.

Managing to look a million more times confident than she felt, Scarlett stepped into the room.

A couple of employees from the music store conversed amiably with Ryan. She overheard Ryan telling them that the audio interface connected to the computer was an integral piece of recording equipment.

From what she could hear above their conversation and the children's playful giggling, Joseph continued to pick out notes on his guitar while half-singing lyrics that were hard to make out. She paused, listening, counting the number of times he used the word *love*.

Yes, he loved the Lord. But this song seemed different. The lyrics sounded like a love song between a man and a woman. The melody was slow, reminding her of a long-ago ballad by Elvis Presley, "Can't Help Falling In Love."

As if sensing her presence, Joseph looked up, and his blue eyes caught her stare. Setting down his guitar, he strode to her.

"Hello, Scarlett." He studied her for a long moment. So long that the familiar flush of hot pink crossed her cheeks.

"Hi, Joseph."

"I'm happy to see you again."

She studied his face for a sign that he was teasing her.

"Not for my singing ability, I assume," she replied. "I don't want to ruin your concerts."

"I bet your voice is lovely." He stepped closer. "As are you."

She glanced down at her disheveled clothes. This close to him, she inhaled his scent of fresh air and a hint of leather.

"Hardly." Self-conscious again, she looked away. "Although I haven't dyed my hair green yet." Her gaze traveled to the ever-present dark stubble on his chin, his thick, wavy hair. Despite the haircut, his hair still curled at the nape.

"I've been reading up on hair dyeing," he said, "and a drastic hair change sometimes means a woman is looking for a transformation in her life."

She lifted her eyebrows. "All that? Can't it just be for a fun change?"

He turned her to face him squarely, placing his hands on her shoulders. "You look great either way."

"Suppose I dyed my hair blue?"

He grinned. "Surprise me." Taking her hand, he led her to the stool next to his.

CHAPTER 5

The next two weeks stretched in front of Joseph in a delightful routine.

Scarlett's part-time schedule at Canine Helpers allowed her to rehearse with him and the children after school. Because Valentine's Day was fast approaching, they spent an hour every weekday practicing.

On Thursday, he met Scarlett at noon and walked with her to the Goodwill store. Winter had tightened its hold on the town, and she was diligent in her efforts to keep every child warmly dressed.

Once inside Goodwill, he insisted on footing the bill for children's coats, scarves, and an array of woolen mittens. He knew Scarlett struggled with finances, as she'd recently lost her full-time job as the receptionist at a veterinary clinic in town.

As they exited the store, he took her gloved hand in his.

Notwithstanding the cold, a pale sun shone overhead, prodding jewel-colored violets to bloom. He snatched a delicate bunch from the ground and handed the flowers to her.

"An early Valentine's gift," he said.

She paused in midstep and sniffed them. "Thank you. They're beautiful." A radiant smile lit her expression.

Her green coat hugged her voluptuous curves, and leopard ear muffs partially covered her lustrous hair. She looked gorgeous, with the brisk air adding a healthy tint to her cheeks.

As he continued to gaze at her lively eyes, her pert nose, her cupid lips, he felt an unexpected melancholy. He would be leaving soon. And he would miss her.

She had such a likable personality, animated and earnest, especially when she smiled. He liked the optimism surrounding her and her patient love for the children.

She exhibited, he thought with an inward sigh of sadness, all the traits he'd been looking for in a woman.

"No one has ever given me flowers before," she said.

"Really? I'm surprised."

She dismissed his comments with a wave. "Your compliments are far too generous."

"On the contrary," he started to say, before she bit her bottom lip and turned away.

He'd pondered what to get her for Valentine's Day, the final day of his concerts. Flowers? Candy? A parting gift? He drew a long, ragged breath. His chest tightened. He couldn't imagine never seeing her again.

"When violets begin to bud," she said, "spring can't be far behind."

Her words carried the realization that a new season was upon them. Spring—rebirth and light, the promise that God's will in nature, and in life, would be done.

Shoulder to shoulder, they continued walking through the park carrying two bags of children's clothing.

"Why did the veterinarian practice close?" he asked.

She kept her gaze straight ahead. Nearby, a young family flew a kite, their toddler racing across the grass and giggling.

"The vet moved away," she finally said.

"And consequently, you were out of a job."

She flinched, but he wasn't sorry for bringing up the subject. "Dorothy mentioned that you and the vet were dating." Actually, Dorothy had told him about Scarlett's broken engagement, but he wanted Scarlett to explain.

She gazed at the kite billowing in the air. "I don't want to burden you with my problems."

"Try me." He beckoned her to sit on a park bench, then slid beside her.

"Judson and I were engaged." With a sigh, she tucked the bags beneath the bench, then fanned the violets carefully beside her. "And then Judson broke the engagement."

"He's a foolish man to let you go," Joseph said.

"He didn't like my personality." She blinked, then shaded her eyes, watching the toddler tumble in the grass. "Rest assured, I'm well over the good doctor," she hastily added.

"Good."

"Why?"

"Because I really like your personality." Joseph slid an arm around her. "And I like *you* a lot."

"Don't go there." Her shoulders stiffened. "My heart is out of reach."

"That's not what I see when we're together." He tipped her face up to him. She was so attractive, although her expression was full of wariness.

"Joseph, I—"

He lowered his head. "Kiss me," he murmured against her lips.

She didn't fight him. Instead, she pressed nearer to him, her mouth meeting his for a long sweet kiss.

When the kiss ended, he rested his chin on her head. She

stirred, and his arms tightened. "Don't move yet," he whispered. "Let's stay like this for a while."

He longed to kiss her again, to have her drive away the ache that filled his chest. As the days had passed, he'd come to realize that his life was now fuller than it had ever been. And his muse had been restored, inspiring him to compose again.

She shifted. "We don't want to be late for your rehearsal."

"I have it on good authority that the rehearsal is being run by an extremely good-natured musician."

She laughed. "Do you happen to know his name?"

They gathered their bags and continued their walk to the Big Brothers Big Sisters building hand in hand. A light dusting of snow began to fall, a wintry reminder, transforming the landscape to a powdery white.

"There go the violets," he said.

"The flowers are hardier than you think. And, besides, this snow won't last. By tomorrow, the sun will come out and melt everything."

SHE'D BEEN CORRECT. The following day, the icicles on the eaves of the shops had melted and the sidewalks were clear.

Daily practices were even better than their walks, Joseph decided. He'd earmarked the stool beside him for Scarlett, encouraging her and the children to belt out the chorus of his worship song in their loudest voices. Admittedly, throughout the rehearsals, he only had eyes for Scarlett.

The following week, Joseph didn't know what to expect when he sprinted into the rehearsal room at exactly 4:00. Normally, he'd meet Scarlett beforehand at Canine Helpers, but he'd accepted a long-distance call from Australia and had texted her to go ahead without him. He hoped she'd managed okay—walking the children to rehearsal, getting them settled and handing out lyrics took a great deal of effort, and she'd admitted to him that she was disorganized.

He rushed into the rehearsal room with his guitar in hand. He'd made record time, dashing from The Cherish Hills Inn to Musically Yours in under fifteen minutes. He'd been in a hurry to finish the phone call so he could see Scarlett.

"A pastor in Australia is requesting a new worship song for the grand opening of their church," he explained. He didn't add that he'd ended the conversation by saying he couldn't commit.

Joseph glanced around the rehearsal room at the children. "Hi everyone."

They giggled, waved, and held up their music.

"We're ready!" Joanna said.

"Joseph, you're out of breath," Scarlett said. "I'll get you a bottle of water."

She had been sitting on a chair next to Joanna and fixing the girl's ponytail. When she got up, he did a double take. Oh, boy. He could gaze at her forever. Her luxurious mane spilled over her shoulders, and her hips swayed as she walked over to the cooler for a water bottle and then brought it to him. She wore a magnificent peach-colored sweater, embellished with a sparkling daisy pin, and a pair of black slacks that outlined her stunning, curvy figure.

He met her halfway. Defying propriety, he placed an arm around her shoulders.

"You look gorgeous," he said.

That figure. Those sea-green eyes. He'd be thinking about her the rest of the evening.

"We are being closely watched by five children," she murmured.

"And I'm merely leading my lovely assistant director to

her rightful place beside me." He kissed her lightly on the forehead, prompting cheers from the children.

Thirty minutes later, they'd reviewed the chorus of his song, "And We Sing, You Are Our God," several times.

"Can I show you something new I've been composing?" he asked.

Encouraged by the chorus of yeses, he plucked the melody on his guitar and then handed the lyrics to Scarlett.

"'The Kingdom Of Heaven Never Stops.'" She glanced at him. "Will you sing it for us?"

He obliged, playing the opening chords. "'No fear. The kingdom of heaven never stops.'" He sang straight through to the final chorus: "'We sing your praise on earth as in heaven.'"

He looked up. The room had stilled and Ryan and Dorothy stood in the doorway. Silently, they applauded before returning to the music store.

"My new favorite song," Scarlett breathed as the children clapped.

"Do you like it?" He grinned.

"I love it."

"Thanks. We'll sing this, and 'You Are Our God' for the concert finale," Joseph said. "Okay?"

"You're only giving us a few days to learn a new song."

"I just finished the melody last night. But I bet if the kids rehearse a few more times, they'll get it. They're professionals. They don't even need musical directors."

"Alright." Scarlett paused. "Dorothy mentioned you were writing two songs. Are you finished with the second one?"

"We won't need that one for the concert. It's … personal." He took a long drink from his water bottle. The song meant too much to him. He wanted to sing it to Scarlett when it was finished. When it was flawless. Like her. "So let's call this rehearsal a wrap and play cards."

"Cards? Play cards? During a children's music rehearsal when you've just given us a new song?"

"A couple more practices and they'll be top-notch." With that, he sat on the floor. Extracting a deck of cards from his duffel bag, he beckoned the children and Scarlett to sit around him.

"Who wants to play Crazy Eights?" he asked, laughing as Joanna raised her hand. He dealt out cards to each child and indicated a brightly wrapped box in his duffel bag to Scarlett. "I found Charlie's Chocolatiers," he whispered.

"Do you just follow around your sweet tooth?"

He winked. "Mostly I just follow around you like it's my profession."

A half hour later, he'd purposely allowed a different child to win each card game, and indulged them by giving out chocolates as prizes.

Scarlett chuckled. "Remember, we are the adults in the room."

"Adults play cards," he replied.

"That's not what I meant. Adults don't make funny faces after each play, or sing silly songs, or stuff three pieces of chocolate in their mouth every five minutes. The kids need to respect you so they'll cooperate with your requests."

"Aren't they cooperating?" he asked.

She shook her head. "Not if you keep acting like a kid."

"Lately, I'd forgotten the sheer joy of just having fun. Some of these children have serious home matters," Joseph said quietly. "Let's keep laughter in their lives."

He'd spoken with Isaac about becoming a mentor, and Isaac had explained that it was a commitment to one child for a year. Joseph's heart grappled with what that meant—a promise, staying in one place. And he'd prayed, waiting for God's answer.

Although what if his prayers weren't about God's response, but more about his own convictions?

"Time's up, kids," Scarlett announced, nudging Joseph and tapping at her watch.

As they stood, Russell raised his hand. "Mr. Slater, where are you from?" he asked.

"A small town in Pennsylvania," Joseph replied.

"Do your mom and dad still live there?"

"No, but my sister does." Joseph held the deck by its sides, and with a light touch, shuffled the cards before stowing them into the case.

"I didn't know you had siblings," Scarlett said.

"Yes. My sister Samantha." Joseph was silent for a moment. "She's a couple years older than me. She's not married, either."

"Where are your parents?" Joanna spoke up, twisting and untwisting the ties of her pink hoodie.

"They're in heaven." Briefly, Joseph smiled. "They passed away when I was a teen."

"Where do you live now?" Joanna again.

"Nowhere." He hesitated, reflecting. "Everywhere."

"You mean you don't have a house?" Russell asked.

"Nope."

With a defeated slump of his shoulders, Russell muttered, "Neither do I." He refused to join Joanna and the other children, now cavorting around the room.

"See what I mean?" Scarlett murmured to Joseph. "No discipline and we'll have chaos on our hands."

Joseph hardly heard her. He was paying particular attention to Russell. Striding over, he took a seat beside him and they chatted quietly for a while.

When Joseph rejoined Scarlett a few minutes later, she asked, "What was that about?"

"Russell is a good kid. I wanted to see if I could help in

any way. It's obvious he's been wounded. I don't know if something happened at home, or at school …"

"That's a roadblock you'll encounter many times," she said. "Home life, lack of two stable parental figures, limited finances. These kids have experienced many hard knocks."

Joseph drew in a quiet breath. Between him and Scarlett, the silence was broken only by the sounds of giggling children, and the heartbreaking sight of one small boy with slumped shoulders and straight black hair sitting alone.

Music blared from the music store, as Dorothy apparently had switched the background recording to a Mozart piano sonata.

"You don't have a home, then?" Scarlett asked.

"I haven't found a place to settle down."

Until now. The thought came to the fore, unbidden.

But didn't he consider himself a Nowhere Man? The name from one of his favorite songs by the Beatles. *He was a real nowhere man.* He glanced at Scarlett, who openly stared at him. As usual, she was in tune with him, although she hadn't said a word.

But was "he making all his nowhere plans for nobody"?

"I want to travel and see the world like you," Joanna declared as she raced by, with the other children happily in pursuit. "I want an exciting, fun life and I want to meet lots of cool people."

Cool people.

Joseph grinned. Scarlett grinned. "She's growing up too fast," they said in unison.

"I never met a stranger," he said to Joanna as she raced past him again. "Just remember no matter how far you travel, keep your family and friends close. And God is most important."

Joanna put her hands on her knees and leaned over to

catch her breath. "You say that because you write worship music."

"God is the center of my heart, and my experiences figure into my songs. What I see, what's occurred in my life, is all part of the song."

As Joanna scampered away, Scarlett asked, "Do you think she got any of that?"

"I hope so."

"Your songs bring tears to my eyes, you know that?" Scarlett said.

"Thank you. That means a great deal coming from you."

"Why? I'm no music critic."

"You're a million times better than any critic because you speak from the heart." He sealed his words with a light kiss on her lips.

At exactly five thirty, Isaac and another mentor arrived to escort the children back to Big Brothers Big Sisters. Scarlett helped with their coats and boots, then bid them goodbye.

"Can I walk you home?" Joseph asked as Scarlett grabbed her coat.

"Sure." She shook back her hair and tied her paisley scarf into a graceful knot at her throat. "I'd like that."

THEY STROLLED HAND IN HAND, covering the easy walk in thirty minutes. At the doorway to her apartment, she wavered. "Would you like to come in?"

"You said you cooked, right?"

"Yes."

"And it's dinnertime."

She regarded her watch. "Yes, it is."

"Then do you remember telling me about a meatloaf recipe your friend, Cathie, gave you, using homemade barbecue sauce?"

"You have an impressive memory." Quickly, Scarlett went over in her mind the food in her refrigerator and pantry. Ground beef and potatoes, lettuce for a salad. "Are you up for mashed potatoes, as long as you peel?"

"Comfort food on a cold February night? Are you kidding? I'll peel a five pound bag."

"You'll only need to peel two pounds for us." She tried to tamp down the little thrill of elation that ran up her spine. After all these days, they'd be sharing their first meal together. Anxiety battled with elation.

They entered her apartment, and she switched on the lamps in the living room. She'd decorated the interior with care, opting for sunny yellow and turquoise throw pillows to offset her orange-checkered sofa and side chair. The coffee table was a miniature wine barrel she'd found at a flea market, and a fluted bowl of fresh oranges sat on the table.

"I love orange," she explained.

"And green hair," he reminded.

"Did you know orange is the color of enthusiasm and joy?"

"I do now," he said with a grin. "And the color fits your personality perfectly."

Her curtains were a pressed gray silk. She'd painted the walls greige, a combination of beige and gray, and a cream-colored carpet completed the airy design.

"Nice place." He took her coat, then shrugged off his own and hung them in her foyer closet. "Your creativity and sense of design is amazing."

It showed in his gaze, his sincere admiration and interest in her, and she smiled as she led him to her tidy, efficient kitchen.

He washed his hands at the sink, then pulled up a stool at the island. "Bring it on. I'm ready to peel."

"After the potatoes are cooked and drained, the recipe calls for sour cream."

He rolled up his sleeves. "I'm liking this dinner better and better."

After handing him a peeler, knife, and empty pan, she set to work making the meatloaf—washing her hands, dicing an onion, and including a loaf of Italian bread to the mix.

"Can I add something for Valentine's Day?" He rose to stand beside her as she spooned the meat into a baking pan.

"Valentine's Day isn't for a while yet," she reminded.

"But we're together now." He shaped the meat mixture into a heart and stepped back.

"Where did you learn how to cook?" she asked.

"Here and there. I've lived alone ever since I went on the road. A guy can't eat take-out every night of the week." He offered a devastating smile.

He was all male. His shoulders seemed strong enough to carry the heaviest burden. He was witty, talented, and generous. And his scent—sweat and brisk air—made her wish he would always be near, that this evening would last forever.

She knew it couldn't. He'd be leaving the day after the concert.

"Plus," he said, "my father always made meatloaf on Valentine's Day for my mother. I remember them laughing in the kitchen while he cooked. My sister and I would peek around the corner of the living room and watch them."

Scarlett set the timer on the oven for one hour. "Your father must have been very romantic. Most men think of just buying flowers and chocolates, or taking a woman to a fancy restaurant."

"Looking back, my father was a romantic. And do you know what happened next?"

She chuckled. "What? Your father burned the meatloaf?"

"Nope. It came out perfect every time."

Joseph brought her into his arms and pressed his lips to hers. "This happened." His hands slid across her shoulders and down her back, pressing her to him. Helpless, she surrendered as he kissed her thoroughly and repeatedly.

Please, don't ever stop, she thought, as she wound her hands around his neck.

Sixty minutes passed, and the meatloaf came out of the oven. She allowed it to cool, then set it on a white stoneware platter.

"Watch this." Grinning, Joseph carefully arranged mashed potatoes around the heart-shaped meatloaf.

They sat at her chrome table in her tiny kitchen, and he offered a prayer of thanks.

One hour later, they'd eaten dinner and cleared the table. Joseph insisted on helping her load the dishwasher, pausing between dishes to nuzzle her neck with a kiss.

She couldn't think beyond the gentle touch of his lips. The sweet tone of his voice as he sang—the Beatles, traditional hymns, a recent pop hit. His tenor voice filled her with optimism. She wanted this, wanted him, every day of her life.

Afterwards, in her cozy living room, he sat beside her on the sofa, legs touching, his arm circled around her.

"I was surprised this afternoon at rehearsal," she began.

"About how well the kids sang?" He pressed a kiss on her temple. He did that often. "Thanks to my excellent assistant director, they're well-rehearsed."

"It's not me. It's you. You have a way with them—a rapport that's innate. They worship you."

"I don't want them to worship me. I want them to worship God."

"I didn't mean it in that way. They look up to you. You're a good role model."

"As are you."

"Joseph." Unwilling to let anything dampen the marvelous

evening, she gave him a reassuring smile before she spoke. "I learned something new about you today. Your tours take you far and wide, but you've managed to keep the relationships that really matter—with your sister Samantha, and with Ryan and Dorothy—close."

"Isn't that the way it's supposed to be?"

"I've always believed that relationships are more grounded if a person stays in one place." She sighed. "I suppose it's because of my father. He's a roamer. And still, after all these years, I can't accept that."

"Are you an only child?"

"Yes." She closed her eyes for an instant. "Unlike you, my father can't be depended on to stay in touch, especially after my mother passed a few years ago. Sometimes it's a few days, sometimes weeks or months go by without a word from him. I get so angry, so frustrated, when he goes dark and won't return my calls."

"You can't change him, Scarlett."

"I know, and I'm sorry."

A puzzled smile touched Joseph's lips. "For what?"

"When I first met you, I compared you to my father."

He frowned. "And that isn't a compliment."

"Sadly, no." She replayed the scenes of her childhood in her mind. "When I was young, I lived in Chicago with my parents. Every time my father was ready to leave, I would tug at his coat and beg him to stay. And then, after he left, I'd count the days until his homecoming." She closed her eyes, could hardly inhale. "The fat girl, staring out the window waiting for her father's return. Pathetic." She glanced at Joseph for his reaction, but his face remained impassive. Still, fearful he might feel sorry for her, she waved her hand airily. "It doesn't matter, of course."

"Did he travel on business?"

"He was a salesman, but he gambled his money. We always struggled financially. Now he drives a rig."

Joseph's arm around her tightened. "And your mother?"

"She never reacted, just always agreed with him." Scarlett's smile was grim. "My mom and I were exact opposites. I questioned him, whereas she stayed silent. 'Why couldn't he stay in one place?' I'd ask her. In my opinion, that's what made a person dependable and trustworthy."

"Strong roots. Staying in one place."

She nodded. "Yes."

"And you shared your opinions with him, also?"

Her gaze clouded as she recalled the distressing scenes —her crying, him walking out the door. "Many, many times."

"So when I saw you with him in the restaurant, he was just passing through Cherish?"

"My father's patented remark—*Just passing through*. He managed to have lunch with me, but when I asked him to stay longer ... Well, he just couldn't, I guess." She blew out a breath. "What causes people to wander?"

"Travel sometimes ignites a hunger for more."

"More what?"

"I'm not sure. Maybe God placed wanderlust in some of us to carry the Gospel." He paused, silently reflective. "Many times at the end of a concert, I'd walk outside and find a quiet place, preferably at the top of a hill. I'd look out over the city, sparkling with lights, and sing a favorite psalm. I'd praise Him. I refused to allow myself to forget that God created everything."

"Joseph, your faith is truly inspiring." She realized she was staring at him with love in her eyes. This exquisite Christian man.

He looked down at her, and his expression of interest, of sincere caring, touched every nerve in her pulse.

"Or sometimes," he said, "we wander because we haven't arrived yet."

"Arrived where?"

"Home." He traced his finger along the curve of her cheekbone. "Home at last."

Softly, she laughed, feeling outrageously elated. With him, she felt safe and loved. Sharing his faith, he'd explained that his sights were set on heaven, but his feet were firmly planted on the ground.

"Cherish is my home," she said.

"And as each day passes, I believe that God brought me here for a reason." He tipped up her chin, looked deeply into her eyes. "I'm a man who strives to tell the truth."

"And the truth is?"

"I believe I am falling in love with you."

Her heart felt like it was beating in triple-time. "It's too soon," she murmured. Her words said one thing, the right thing, but her emotions felt another.

"Not if it's meant to be. I'm hoping you're feeling what I'm feeling."

She was, but she couldn't tell him, for soon he'd be gone. She stroked her fingers against the ever-present stubble on his chin. "I care for you, but we don't know each other well."

He smiled. "So you've said." He seemed to accept her explanation, although he cocked a dark eyebrow as he spoke.

How could he believe her protests, when she didn't believe them herself?

His lips brushed against hers. "Can you admit you're as happy as I am?"

"Yes. Extremely happy." She attempted to smile, but tears blurred her vision.

Gently, he cupped her face between his fingers, and his thumb stroked an errant tear from her cheek. "So why are you crying?"

"Because you're a good man and—"

She left it at that as he kissed her.

He was a man who deserved a confident, slim woman by his side. And she deserved someone who would be there for her, not on some Skype screen halfway around the world.

Still, she snuggled into his embrace as she dashed the tears from her eyes and pondered his words.

Effectively, he had spun a new meaning to the term *wanderlust*. He'd proved there could be positive aspects to a life lived lightly rather than deeply grounded.

His path had taken him one way, hers another.

And perhaps either way was good.

CHAPTER 6

*A*s she did every morning, Scarlett walked to her job at Canine Helpers. The days with Joseph had delightfully blended together, and there was a decided spring to her step.

Her cell phone chirped, and she recognized the caller ID.

"Good morning, Dorothy," she answered.

"All three Valentine performances are sellouts," Dorothy said. "Friday and Saturday nights, and the Sunday matinee. Isn't that remarkable for such a small town? Ryan and I discussed a Sunday evening performance, but it is Valentine's Day and all."

"And all what?" Scarlett asked. "You and Ryan want to celebrate the holiday?"

"Not us. We're newlyweds and know we'll be together."

"Uh-huh." Scarlett expelled a long breath. "And?"

"And, well, you might want to spend the evening with a certain famous musician. Maybe dinner at a fancy restaurant, discussing your future, holding hands … Whatever two people in love might do."

"Two people in love?" Scarlett parroted. She blinked, massaged her temple.

Dorothy sniffed, an all-knowing sniff. "Your attraction to Joseph is written all over your face. On his too."

"Is it that obvious?" Scarlett blurted, and then quickly closed her mouth. But really, what did Dorothy see?

Love.

"The entire town is buzzing about how you two are so good together. In church this past Sunday, you held hands during most of the service. And word is that Joseph met with Isaac about becoming a mentor."

"He did?" Scarlett had reached the center of town. She paused to eye the shop windows, the traditional red and white Valentine designs festive and eye-catching.

"Didn't he tell you?" Dorothy asked. "I assumed that by now you two were sharing everything."

"No, as a matter of fact, he didn't mention meeting with Isaac."

This was completely new territory, and Scarlett wondered why Joseph hadn't spoken about it, especially because mentoring meant so much to her. But then, since he'd arrived, everything had happened so rapidly, coupled with the powerful feelings he ignited in her, that she'd barely had time to comprehend their chemistry. She just reveled in it.

"You're reading too many romance novels," she said. "Life doesn't work that way and Joseph is committed to perform in several major cities. He's leaving on Monday for Raleigh, and I'm sure he'll have a list of things to do before he checks out of the inn."

And he was checking out of her life. Any hope she'd clung to that he might stay had promptly disappeared with the passing days when he hadn't mentioned a future they might have together.

"You know him, but I know him too," Dorothy said. With that, she clicked off before Scarlett could ask, "What's that supposed to mean?"

Before she could harbor any false expectations, she dismissed fanciful dreams from her mind. There were Big Brothers Big Sisters organizations in numerous major cities, and Joseph could mentor a different child in each.

No. No he couldn't. The organization wanted a one-year commitment. So there went that idea.

Still, Joseph had hinted that he'd like their relationship to continue, although he hadn't come out and made a specific plan. Sure, they talked constantly—about nothing and every-thing, like what time of year bluebonnets were in full bloom, their favorite ice cream flavors at Whitney's, (hers was peanut butter crunch, his butter pecan although he preferred the candy store), and the benefits of eating dark chocolate versus milk chocolate.

And always the conversation swerved to encompass his music and songs, her passion for animals, her love for Joanna and how proud she was of her accomplishments. Much to everyone's delight, Joanna was excelling in her harp lessons —already reading music and practicing a measure at a time (as Emmanuelle had instructed) on a small harp Dorothy had lent her for home use.

In the evenings after rehearsals, Scarlett and Joseph would walk to her apartment, stopping at the grocer to buy fresh, nutritional ingredients for dinner. He'd insist on buying a bouquet of flowers—cheerful daisies with a button center, or rainbow-colored carnations, or an array of large golden sunflowers—and he'd arrange them in a large glass vase in the middle of her kitchen table.

After dinner, their non-stop talks went on until late in the evening. For a midnight snack, she'd brew a pot of herbal tea, along with toasted slices of whole grain bread topped with local honey.

He spoke of his travels, embellishing his descriptions about the lush greenery of Ireland, or the high-rises in New York City, or the natural beauty of an Australian beach. And his stories of those places made her yearn to travel, which surprised her.

Her. The homebody, who had vowed she'd never leave the safe, stable confines of Cherish.

This is risky, I'm endangering my heart, she'd think, as he thrummed melodies on his guitar—some old, some new, some happy, some sad. She knew that no matter where he journeyed, after he left he would take a piece of her heart with him.

On his cell phone, he'd shot various selfies of them at Musically Yours, in front of Canine Helpers, and loads of photos with Joanna. He had developed many of the shots into large colorful photos and hung them on Scarlett's living room walls. In one particular photo of Joseph and Russell, taken in front of Isaac's office, Russell held a blue balloon proclaiming "Happy Birthday," as it had been Isaac's birthday that day. Joseph, dressed as usual in jeans and a T-shirt that proclaimed *God is Love*, had his arm firmly around Russell's shoulders. Both smiled into the camera.

"I care so much about these kids," Joseph had said when he'd hung that picture. He took Scarlett into his arms. "Almost as much as I care about you."

A shiver went through her as he held her close. She tried to make light of his remark by giving her standard answer: "We don't know each other well enough yet."

"I know all I need to know about you," he refuted.

"It's necessary to date a person a certain length of time before anything serious can develop," she said.

"How long?"

"Obviously, longer than a few weeks. There are certain rules, Joseph."

He shrugged. "I've never been a follower of rules."

She smiled, liking the sound of that. She'd wanted to press her cheek against the soft cotton of his shirt and declare that she'd never cared for rules, either.

Please stay. But she said nothing.

Hopefulness was a funny thing. It could break your heart quicker than anything else. Tear a person apart. And she couldn't hinge her dreams on a man who was here today, gone tomorrow.

He'd also made sizable donations to both Canine Helpers and Big Brothers, and word had spread quickly throughout the town of Joseph's generosity.

Therefore, the weeks since he'd first set foot in Cherish had been the best weeks of Scarlett's life. So much, that on the Thursday morning before the concert weekend, she grappled with surges of despondency and the stark realization that time was passing much too quickly.

At noon, Joseph met her on the steps of Canine Helpers. Neatly dressed in his favorite pair of dark-washed jeans, a graphic T-shirt that said *God Is with Us*, and his black leather jacket, he was impossibly handsome. She felt exhilarated, and smiled at the utter delight of seeing him.

He set down his duffel bag and enveloped her in his arms. "Today," he said, "we are going out to lunch."

"We can't." She patted her waistline. "I'm on a—"

He put a finger to her lips, opened his duffel, and extracted a brown bag. "I figured you'd say that. So I bought a salad at The Garden Terrace for you, and two slices of lemon cake for me."

"Two slices? Do you know how many calories are in a slice of lemon cake? If the second piece is for me—"

"The choice is yours. If you don't eat it, I will." He shook the bag. "The restaurant gave us plastic forks and bottles of water too."

"We were going back to the Goodwill store this afternoon, remember?"

He made a show of shading his eyes and staring at the vibrant Carolina sky. "You predicted the snow would melt. It did. And the kids now own so many gloves and hats that they could trek across the Arctic Circle and never be cold."

"It's February. More snow could easily be coming."

"We'll take our chances." With a flash of white teeth, he favored her with a charming grin. "At the restaurant I asked which salad is your favorite, and the waitress with spiked hair said that last time you ordered a Cobb salad and didn't finish it."

Scarlett laughed. "Now why would you go through all that trouble?"

He gazed at her for a long moment, drew her into his arms, and said in a velvety voice, "Surely you know why."

Her heart hammered wildly while caution screamed in her ears. *Don't risk it. A few more days and he'll be gone.*

She stepped away and whispered frantically, "Please don't look at me like that."

He stepped an inch forward and kept his hands at his side. "Also, I wanted to thank you for your help," he said softly. "Without you, I never would have been able to pull this concert off."

"I highly doubt it, but I'll accept your compliment." Considering, she stared at Canine Helpers—the covered walkway, the squat wooden exterior, the small forested area in the back. "The waitress remembered I didn't finish the salad?" she asked.

"Small towns. Everybody knows everything about everyone."

She burst out laughing. "You're 100 percent correct."

"I'm starting to like small-town life." He kissed her hair. "So we can play hooky today."

"What does liking a small town have to do with playing hooky?"

"Absolutely nothing." He stated it with such conviction, she didn't know how to dispute his reasoning. Shaking the bag again, he asked, "Lunch it is?"

"We can't." So much for not disputing him. "The kids will be disappointed."

"They won't arrive at Big Brothers until after school." This close, the warmth of his body made her feel like nothing could ever go wrong in their world. The faint scent of his leather jacket tingled her nostrils, causing her pulse to quicken. "And just in case, I phoned Isaac and informed him we might be a little late."

"As usual, you took care of everything."

He gestured toward a hill past the park. "You look gorgeous in that fuchsia blouse, by the way. I like you in the red family."

"Red family?"

"You know, red, pink, rose."

"The colors are a family?"

He grinned boyishly. "Why not?"

She laughed at his logic and studied him as they walked.

When the time comes, accept that he'll leave and don't cling to him. Be grateful for the affection you've received.

In the midst of sunshine and breezes full of expectation, he took her hand. His grip was strong and reassuring, bringing her comfort.

She tossed him a light-hearted smile. "Did you know I've lost five pounds?"

"I do, because you've mentioned it a half dozen times. And I always respond the same way— you don't need to diet. You're perfect."

"Skinny is considered the epitome of attractiveness."

"That's ridiculous."

"You're being very kind. But thanks." Despite her shrug, she smiled, his compliment warming her insides.

* * *

AS THEY KEPT WALKING, Joseph couldn't stop himself from openly admiring Scarlett. The vivacious smile he'd come to appreciate, the freckles on her cheeks, the bright colors she wore—which today was that fuchsia blouse and matching slacks beneath her green coat. Shimmery green earrings dangled from her delicate ears, the color of emeralds, fault-lessly matching her glorious eyes.

Everything about her was exceptional. Her appearance always eye-catching and somewhat outrageous, his Scarlett.

His Scarlett?

He couldn't help grinning as they walked hand in hand.

He opened his mouth to begin a conversation, then closed it. The Lord had taught him that it mattered where he started a conversation and where he ended it. Although he'd posi-tioned his life around God, he'd also targeted his life around, well, himself. And *self* was a small focus to center on in such a big world. The realization that he needed more, needed her, was beginning to make absolute sense.

And so he'd planned this excursion for several reasons. Of course he wanted to spend as much time as possible with her before he departed. But there was another reason. He wanted to test his feelings about bringing their relationship to a deeper level—without the babble of pudgy-faced children, or in the midst of peeling potatoes, or within the confines of a noisy rehearsal room.

Wind plucked at the ever-present paisley scarf tucked around her throat. A flame of red hair, the whisper of her laughter, a jangle of shiny silver bangles on her wrist. Everything reminded him of Scarlett, because she had pervaded his senses until he could think of little else.

Did he want to develop their relationship on a deeper level?

Most definitely.

Because lately he could only focus on one thing. He wanted her. He wanted to spend every day, every night, with her.

In this scenic town, they'd embrace a simpler lifestyle, joining close friends at church, as they had every Sunday since he'd arrived. He'd grown to love the pastors, particularly Marge Addyson. Marge was also a mentor at Big Brothers and spent several days a week with Savannah, a troubled teenage girl from a broken family.

Marge was a knowledgeable woman with a rollicking laugh, often showering Joseph and Scarlett with shrewd observations.

"Seeing you two holding hands makes me as happy as a bouquet of bluebonnets in the spring," she had teased them after church last Sunday. "You belong together." As Scarlett had blushed gorgeously, Marge had fixed him with a laser-sharp gaze. "If you don't stay in Cherish, you'll never forgive yourself."

He'd laughed. On the church steps, they had all laughed.

But Marge Addyson had known.

He was in love with Scarlett. And he had told her in a thousand subtle ways, hadn't he?

He squeezed his eyes shut, sending up a silent prayer. *God, what should I do when second thoughts invade my happiness?*

Would he truly be content in a town this size? He knew Scarlett wouldn't be happy moving from one city to another. She wanted permanency and sameness, the security of building a family and living in one place.

They strolled through town, remarking on the shop windows exquisitely decorated for Valentine's Day. He guided her into the local florist and admired the artfully arranged designs—pink azaleas and long-stemmed roses in crystal vases, lavender daisies and white lilies with intense, fragrant blooms.

"Do you have a favorite flower?" he asked. He planned on surprising her with a festive bouquet after the final concert on Sunday.

"The roses are beautiful," she replied, complimenting the shop owner, who was dressed in jeans and a white blouse, an embossed apron draped over her slim body. "But I prefer handpicked flowers, and gifts that come from the heart."

He got it and knew better than to say anything, fearful he would spoil the Valentine surprise he had in store for her.

They exited and continued their stroll.

They discovered a broad winding path and wandered to a sun-dappled gazebo. Setting down his duffel bag, he steered her inside. The gazebo allowed them a limited amount of privacy.

He braced his hands on her shoulders and turned her to face him. Slowly, his head descended, his lips brushing against hers.

"Joseph—" Her voice was unsteady. "Here?"

"Kissing you on this beautiful day is perfectly acceptable. I have it on good authority the townspeople would approve."

Softly, she laughed. "Which townspeople, exactly?"

"Dorothy and Ryan," he said agreeably. "And Isaac and Marge Addyson. And Joanna. You mentioned she was a romantic."

Scarlett chuckled. "That awesome memory of yours again."

He drew her into his arms, and she tipped her head up for

a kiss. Moments later, without warning, she broke the kiss and stepped back.

He took her hands in his and regarded her. "Anything the matter?"

She glanced at the hill beyond, her expression solemn. "We should get going."

Quietness punctuated a lengthy moment.

"Okay." He tried to reply as impersonally as she had. He picked up his duffel bag and they continued at a quicker pace.

However odd her response, it was heaven to clasp his hand around hers, to be in a comfortable, Godly place without the barriers of travel and suitcases and exhaustion.

So what if she was quieter than normal? Women were quiet sometimes, weren't they?

When they arrived at the top of the hill, the view provided a picturesque expanse of the town. The sky provided a celebration of brilliant sunshine, and birdsong drifted from the trees. Beside him, Scarlett amiably responded to his questions about becoming a mentor.

He was surprised she didn't pry him for more details, but she didn't. Instead, she inserted stories about Joanna and Joanna's mother and siblings.

As Scarlett spoke with animation, he pictured her as a little girl growing up in big-city Chicago, her hair in red pigtails, carrying a pink lunchbox, skipping to school. And then going home, filled with confidence and its counterpart, uncertainty, wondering if her father would be there.

"I've packed everything for our picnic," he said. "Right down to …" He pulled out a blanket he'd stuffed in his duffel bag and spread it on the cool grass. They sat and ate the feast he'd provided, her salad and his lemon cake, and washed the food down with bottles of water.

When they'd finished, he pulled his gaze from the familiar scene of the town park.

"Let's go behind the railroad tracks," he suggested.

She sent him a wry look. "Excuse me?"

"Ryan showed me where he and Dorothy used to slingshot when they were kids. Apparently, Dorothy was exceptionally good."

Scarlett laughed. "If you're gauging my abilities with a slingshot against Dorothy's, you'll be sorely disappointed."

"I don't carry one myself, so you're in luck. And I doubt I could ever beat Ryan, anyway."

She smiled, then eyed her wristwatch and stood. "High time we get to Big Brothers. It's almost three o'clock."

"I told Isaac—"

"Yes, but we don't want to be late. This afternoon is the final rehearsal before the concert tomorrow evening."

"Don't you want to spend our last hours alone together?" He attempted to keep his feelings in check—annoyance, disappointment, wanting her to explain why she didn't want to prolong the moment of being alone in this exquisite place.

"Joseph, we've spent the past three hours together. Isn't that enough?" She pursed her lips. The sharp tang of her remark cut through him.

He stiffened. "Sorry to waste your time."

She grabbed their belongings and began walking. "Don't be ridiculous."

"I'm leaving Monday morning." He hastened to keep up with her. "Shouldn't we talk about it?"

She slowed and gazed at him. Her beautiful eyes darkened with an emotion he couldn't read.

"Why? What is there to say?" she asked softly. He was surprised when the shrug she offered seemed somewhat indifferent. He'd expected a warmer response—a fervent *Yes, how can we arrange a long-distance relationship?* Or, *Have you considered staying in Cherish?*

"I'm thinking about becoming a mentor," he said.

"So I heard. I wondered why you didn't say anything when I was going on and on about Joanna."

It took a Herculean effort not to ask her why she hadn't mentioned anything to him. Of course, he hadn't mentioned anything to her, either, but that was because it was an idea—one based on prayer and faith and love—but still only an idea.

He shot her a quizzical glance. "I assumed you would be excited."

"I am. Good luck with it. I'm sure you'll find mentoring rewarding."

He waited for her to ask where he planned to mentor—in Cherish, in New York, in Atlanta ...

"That's it?" he asked.

"I wished you luck. Should I add *safe travels?*"

"I'm not flying off to the moon." Slowly, he reached for her hand.

She pulled back. "Australia is almost as far."

"Our time together has just begun, Scarlett."

He wanted her to agree. *Assumed* she would agree.

She hesitated, tightening her green coat around her. "You and I must be on a different time frame. Our time together is ending."

Right.

Wrong.

His mind stopped working. He couldn't counter with a snappy comeback. He could feel her withdrawing further and further away and he didn't know how to bring her back.

"Is that what you want?" He stopped short. "We've continuously had fun together."

"Yes, it's been fun."

It's been fun but ... The word hung silently in the air between them.

And she hadn't answered his question.

"I think it's better," she said slowly, "if I don't join you for tonight's rehearsal."

"Why? What about the concert?"

"You said yourself the kids are so good they don't need a musical director, so they certainly don't need an assistant musical director."

"Now you're the one being ridiculous because you refuse to talk about it."

She winced and met his gaze straight on. "Talk about what?"

"You don't get what I've been trying to tell you all afternoon?"

"Apparently I don't." She took a deep breath and swung her gaze to the florist shop's window. All this time, they'd been walking toward town. He'd hardly noticed.

"And you know what else?" he challenged. "Perhaps that's what you've wanted all along. Me to leave. Perhaps that's what has made me so appealing to you."

"Well, you should know, because you've become such an expert about me in a short amount of time," she lashed out.

"Scarlett." He put his hands on her forearms. "Let's face it. This isn't about me, or even us. It's about you and your absentee father. And your absurd notion that a home has to be in one place or else it doesn't count."

He was spot on. He could see it from the wounded expression on her face—just before she spun from him and stormed away.

CHAPTER 7

On Friday afternoon, Scarlett phoned Dorothy to explain that she wouldn't be able to help with the concerts after all. She added a sincere apology.

"Are you sick?" Dorothy questioned.

Frantically attempting to think of an excuse, Scarlett mumbled through a *not exactly*.

"Okay. Hope you feel better soon."

Dorothy was so caught up in the concert preparations, eager to discuss erecting a tent at the park in case of rain, the chair set-up for the audience, the recording gear and portable outdoor heaters, that their conversation was brief.

"Ryan is saying the sound equipment just arrived," Dorothy said. "And we hired two catering vans to serve refreshments. And security. I'd better tell Nicholas to get on that."

"It's good to have connections with the town deputy," Scarlett murmured. With a final *Good luck*, she clicked off.

Next, she reviewed her conversation with Joanna before she telephoned. As Scarlett expected, Joanna's mother answered. When Joanna insisted on talking, Scarlett offered up a brief apology, saying she wasn't able to attend the Valentine concerts.

Nonetheless, she told Joanna she and the other children would be great. "Break a leg," she added.

"Huh?" Joanna asked.

"That's show-biz talk for good luck."

"Breaking a leg is good luck?"

"It's a theater superstition. If you wish a person good luck, it really means bad luck."

"Huh?" Joanna asked again.

"Don't worry about it. Just have fun."

"Then you aren't coming to any of the concerts?"

Scarlett swallowed, knowing her voice was heavy with unshed tears. "No."

"Why not? Are you sick?"

"I'm okay."

"Are you faking because you're avoiding Mr. Slater? He was great at rehearsal yesterday, but seemed, I don't know, kinda sad somehow. Did you guys have an argument?" In her usual straightforward way, Joanna had zeroed in on the fact.

"Some things are better a certain way, and I know the concerts will be a huge success." Scarlett struggled for composure—to be the adult Joanna knew and respected. But as hard as she tried, she'd let the girl down this time and there was no hope for it. "I'll see you after school on Monday at Big Brothers, okay? I love you."

"I love you too. And Mr. and Mrs. Edwards are taping the concert to make into DVDs, so don't forget to buy one, okay?"

"I won't." Scarlett fidgeted with the tie on her terry cloth robe. "Sing well."

"Sure." With a resigned huff, Joanna clicked off.

Scarlett reassured herself that there were other people to

help with the children—Dorothy and Ryan, Emmanuelle and Nicholas. And of course, Isaac.

Now it was Saturday. Forty-four hours had passed since her argument with Joseph, and those days had been a blur. Her life had lingered in another place, another time, and refused to move forward. Every thought led back to one man.

Joseph. The first time he sang about love and peace in front of Musically Yours, expertly thrumming his guitar. And signing his autograph. *Here you go, two t's, Scarlett.*

Joseph, after finishing his new song, boyishly, expectantly watching for her reaction.

Joseph, waiting patiently for her in front of Canine Helpers. *Today, we are going out to lunch.* He'd respected her diet, asking the waitress which salad Scarlett preferred.

He'd phoned several times in those forty-four hours. He'd texted too. And she hadn't responded because, really, what would she say?

Goodbye? They'd already traveled that road.

Come Friday he'd repeated his calls and texts. She'd vacillated, staring at her cell phone and asking herself: Should I answer?

On the one hand, she knew she should. She wasn't the type of person to leave someone hanging. An argument could only be settled when two people talked openly and agreed to disagree.

On the other hand, what good would it do? He traveled all over the globe and she wouldn't accompany him, although his descriptions of exciting locales had called up a sense of adventure in her.

All good, although the truth was she couldn't handle living on the road. Her life in Cherish had been carefully built, and she wouldn't tear it down to follow a musician who never settled in one place longer than a few weeks. Of course, he also hadn't asked her to come with him. Nor had he said that he would stay.

Don't think about his handsome face, his kind eyes, his full lips.

Sadly, that was all she wanted to do.

Twice, she had reached for her cell phone to call him. Then she reminded herself that she couldn't endanger her heart again. Not even for him. If they did continue their relationship and she chose not to accompany him, she'd share her life with a man who was hardly ever around.

Never again would she be forced to stare out an apartment window, waiting for a man's return.

I yearn for you like crazy, although I refuse to wear rose-colored glasses. You're here, there, and everywhere. I'm in one place, where I intend to stay.

Still, she missed him more than anything, and compulsively replayed all the good things that had occurred between them.

In many ways, her weeks with him had been transformative. He'd forced her to face her feelings about loneliness and loss, about people leaving her life for purely selfish reasons and through no fault of her own, and to accept and forgive them anyway for being who they were. She'd been upset and incensed at Joseph's parting remark, but his words had niggled at her.

This isn't about me, or even us. It's about you and your absentee father. And your absurd notion that a home has to be in one place or else it doesn't count.

Blowing out a sharp sigh, she opened the living room window and let in a waft of air scented with evergreens. The February weather had been undecided, but today was a lovely spring-like day. The sunshine brought a glow, the grass a sparkling green, and new warmth promised wildflowers and tiny buds appearing on the trees.

She padded into her small kitchen and set a kettle on the stove for tea.

A cardinal hopped onto her windowsill, its feathers the color of crimson.

"Hi, little fella," she cooed.

The cardinal nervously flicked its eyes toward her and flew away.

Not once in the last two days had she cried, knowing that crying about a successful musician whom she'd never see again would turn her into an emotional faucet. However, in doing so, she had stored up a horrendous weight of emotion. A sweet bird who preferred to fly away rather than look at her was the final straw.

Tears welled, and she dabbed at her eyes. "Joseph Slater, don't you dare turn me into a blubbering fool." As tears streamed down her cheeks anyway, she poured her tea and went into the living room. Settling on the sofa, she drew her knees up to her chest and wept.

When there were no tears left, she wiped her eyes, perched her chin on her hands, and glanced at her watch. The hours had dragged; showing only midafternoon. Would it always be like this without him? The days long and desolate?

She did what any fat girl would do. She got dressed, went to town, and purchased a quart of peanut butter crunch ice cream at Whitney's, adding a slice of chocolate fudge from Charlie's Chocolatiers. Swinging the bags, she went back to her apartment.

Since Joseph had arrived in Cherish, she'd lost several pounds and was at a weight she hadn't seen since high school. Their nightly dinners included healthy entrées and nutritious appetizers. She'd stuck to her diet and eaten no desserts, save for local honey on toasted bread at midnight.

That was then. This was now.

She'd always used food to tide her over when she'd had a particularly trying day—after the breakup with her fiancé, when she'd felt anxious about her new job at Canine Helpers, pretty much whenever she needed comfort. Stress eating. Emotional eating. Because comfort food, which unfortunately was mostly sugary and processed, made her feel better.

She sat on the sofa and opened the ice cream container.

With the first spoonful halfway to her mouth, she caught the glimmer of sunshine outside her window, the sky dotted with fluffy white clouds.

She paused.

What was she doing, about to gorge on ice cream on this fine Saturday afternoon? After all the weeks of dieting, did she really want to sabotage her weight loss with ice cream and candy?

She fell back against the sofa and closed her eyes.

No, not this time. Making smart, daily choices was the way to wellness. She could banish the word *diet* from her vocabulary, because no magic diet would help her reach her goals. The entire process was solely up to her.

It was big, this change in her mindset, and she realized it. Had she always looked to food for consolation?

Certainly.

But no more.

She placed the ice cream container back in the freezer, the spoon in the dishwasher, the candy in the cupboard, and decided to check out the Saturday service at Memorial Street Church. Normally, she attended on Sunday morning, but there were two excellent reasons why Saturday evening was better.

First, Joseph, Dorothy and Ryan wouldn't be there, as they would be preparing for the concert. So there'd be no awkwardness, no avoiding people, no uncomfortable questions.

Second, Saturday offered a new contemporary service. Chances were good she wouldn't run into anyone except groups of teenagers.

When early evening approached, dusk washed across the sidewalks as Scarlett walked to church. The service proved inspiring and energetic, the pastor's words adding layers of meaning about forgiveness and obedience to God.

When it ended at seven, she slipped from the pew and headed to the exit at the back of the church.

"Scarlett? Is that you?" Marge Addyson's cultured southern voice stopped her. "What are you doing in church tonight?"

Scarlett swiveled, "Hi, Mrs. Addyson. Umm, right. I usually attend on Sunday morning."

Marge's proper pumps clattered across the aisle. For an older woman, she was spry and well-kept. As usual, her gray hair was perfectly coiffed. "What I mean is, I heard you weren't present for last night's concert because you were so sick you needed three beds."

"Is that what you heard?" Scarlett grinned and pressed a greeting kiss to Marge's rouged cheek.

The woman smiled back and tugged on the jacket of her powder-blue wool suit. "I missed you. We all did."

"I'm sure the music was lovely," Scarlett said, congratulating herself on how well she had sidestepped Marge's questions.

"The children were delightful. And that musician of yours has a dreamy, raspy voice that could melt butter. The last worship song—that new one—had everyone on their feet weeping during the finale."

"Yes, I've heard it and it's beautiful." The remembrance

brought a well of emotion bubbling to the surface, and Scarlett dashed tears from her eyes, hoping Marge wouldn't notice. "We're not together anymore."

"You were the ideal couple. What happened?" Marge extended her arms, and Scarlett moved into the bear-hug embrace. Something within her wanted to burst open, to tell the elderly woman everything.

"It's a long story."

"The church is empty." Marge gestured to a pew in the back.

They sat in silence for several beats. Scarlett focused on an arched stained-glass window highlighting a full-length angel, the muted colors glowing as pure silver.

Never quiet for long, Marge nudged Scarlett's shoulder. "I'm a good listener, as well as a good talker, you know. Give me a try."

Scarlett wiped her hands on her pencil skirt. Firmly, determinedly, she fought to control the thickness in her throat as she explained Joseph's kindness, how good he was to her, his rolling-stone lifestyle. All the highs, all the lows. She spoke until there was nothing left to say.

"Dorothy's told me and half the town that you and Joseph are in love," Marge said.

"Has she now?" Scarlett felt a warm blush stain her cheeks as she recalled Joseph's lips moving tenderly on hers.

Don't move yet, he'd whispered. *Let's stay like this for a while.*

"And cute little Joanna told me the same thing when I mentored Savannah a few days ago."

"Joanna is a romantic." Scarlett shook her head. "And Dorothy. Well, Dorothy—"

"Knows you and Joseph well. So your stories about how kind Joseph is, how he opens doors for you and stands when you enter a room, leave out the most important part." Marge took Scarlett's cold hands in her own. "He loves you, and you love him. Everyone else realizes it. Now it's time for you to realize and do something about it."

Scarlett's stomach gave a funny lurch. "Like what?"

"Show up at the concert. There's still an hour left before it starts at eight." Marge tapped at her watch. For the first time, Scarlett noticed the dirt beneath Marge's fingernails. She'd taken up indoor gardening, planting a few tender seedlings. Knowing Marge, she would have the most beautiful garden in Cherish come summer.

"I can't. Not tonight," Scarlett said. "There's something I … Well, I'm making an appointment to go somewhere tomorrow morning."

"After your appointment, then. I'll be there because Ryan invited me to say the blessing before the concert." Marge placed an age-spotted hand on Scarlett's cheek. "You're a vivacious beautiful woman and full of life. Joseph is lucky to have you."

"Hardly." Self-doubt poked through. "He can have anyone. A sweet skinny woman would be able to—"

"He wants you just the way you are. You're foolish if you let a good Christian man leave your life without fighting for him. Go. And be sure to sit in the first row where he can see you. Be a blessing and an encouragement."

And there was the challenge. Hastily, Scarlett nodded, promising Marge before she lost courage. Only her hurt pride had prevented her from making the first move. And if she didn't reach out, Joseph would leave Cherish believing she didn't care about him, and nothing was further from the truth.

"Scarlett, one more thing, and it's the most important." Marge stood and pulled on a pair of tan leather gloves. "Ask

God to lead your heart and mind. The Lord wants you to be happy."

A smile touched Scarlett's lips. She had come to church. She had met Marge. Surely the Lord's hand was in this. With His blessing and her friends' support, she could do this. Besides, she couldn't imagine her future without Joseph.

ON SUNDAY MORNING, Scarlett rose early although she hadn't fallen asleep until dawn. When the alarm rang, she sprang to a sitting position, hurtling from a bottomless dream to full wakefulness in five seconds.

"I can't do it," she whispered to the empty room. Marge had given the worst advice ever.

Of course you can. Just swing your legs over the side of the bed, shower, and get dressed.

Bundled in her terry cloth robe, she deliberated on her wardrobe choices. Cute clothes had always been a problem because of her size, although Joseph had complimented her on everything she'd worn.

She dressed with great care in a pink silk blouse that tied at the waist, black slacks, and animal print pumps sporting a kitten heel. It was Valentine's Day, after all. A bright rosy lipstick, red crystal drop earrings, and Joanna's harp bracelet completed the ensemble. Although the weather promised temperatures in the high fifties, she donned her green wool coat for extra warmth.

Then she texted her hairdresser, Phyllis, convincing her friend to pay back the favor from when Scarlett had helped her move into her new apartment. She made an appointment for eleven o'clock.

With a fluttery feeling in her stomach, she pushed back her shoulders and began a fast-paced stride to Cherish Styles and Clips. First the hairdresser, then the concert. The important thing was that she and Joseph would meet again, face to face. It was so simple, and all she had to do was look him in the eye and tell him how much she loved him.

At one o'clock, Scarlett emerged from the hair salon. The sky was a soft blue, the clouds drifting across it in slow motion. Chirping birds circled in languid arcs, while Scarlett joined the throngs of people headed for the 2:00 matinee. Outside the white canvas tent where the concert would be held, Emmanuelle chatted with Nicholas, holding their golden retriever, Molly Belle, by her leash.

The couple waved gaily to Scarlett and she grinned a hello. She'd reached the park in record time.

She went straight for the back-stage area and placed her coat on a chair.

"You made it!" Joanna exclaimed. "My mom came to the performance last night, and now you're here." She wore a pleated black skirt and white shirt, her hair pulled back in a neat ponytail, and her almond-shaped eyes shone with excitement. "And I love your hair! And your bracelet is awesome, just like mine." She jingled her harp bracelet, prompting Scarlett to do the same, and then nudged Russell. "I told you she wouldn't disappoint us. You owe me a dollar."

The boy elbowed her back. "No, I don't. Anyway, I don't have a dollar." He looked young and vulnerable, an oversized pair of black dress pants and freshly pressed white shirt overpowering his slight frame.

The moment Dorothy came around the corner, her gaze riveted on Scarlett. "Thank goodness you're here. Isaac is running late—some crisis at Big Brothers—and Ryan needs my help with the microphones. Can you watch the children backstage?" She indicated a row of chairs.

"I'm more than happy to help," Scarlett replied.

"Oh, and for the finale, the children are singing twice, the final number being Joseph's new worship song. Do you remember it?"

Scarlett drew a quiet sigh. How could she forget? "His lyrics are so inspirational, I hardly took a breath while he sang."

Ryan came backstage with Marge Addyson. "Are we ready to begin?" he asked Dorothy, giving her a quick hug. "Thanks for organizing all this, my love."

Dorothy grinned. "Happy Valentine's Day."

What would it be like to have a man love a woman so much that he put her before any other goals in his life? Scarlett wondered. Seeing their interaction caused a flash of longing in her heart. She was truly happy for them, as their romance hadn't come about without trials. At the same time, their joy only expanded her own aloneness.

Marge patted Scarlett's arm. "I'm glad you're here."

Scarlett took a deep breath. "Me too." She paused, then turned. Joseph's voice came from the stage as he spoke with one of the sound technicians, followed by the familiar strum of his guitar as he warmed up. Tenderness flooded her heart. She couldn't wait to talk with him again.

She waded into the middle of another disagreement between Joanna and Russell, separated them, and sat them in a row with the other children. Then she peeked around the curtain to catch a glimpse of Joseph.

At 2:00, Marge and Ryan took the stage. Joseph stood in one corner as Ryan invited Marge to offer the opening prayer.

"Thank you, Ryan, for the privilege of praying with all of you." The epitome of poise and elegance, Marge bowed her head and clasped her hands together, requesting the audience to do the same. "Dear Lord, thank you for this fine

February day. We are grateful that every seat for this concert has been filled. Bless all those present, and may the uplifting music fill our hearts and ears as we worship you in song. Amen."

After Dorothy seated Marge in the front row, Ryan continued. Engaging and relaxed, he spoke to the crowd with enthusiasm, wished everyone a happy Valentine's Day and thanked them for their support. He then expounded on the benefits of expanding the elementary school's music program.

"Music allows children to build self-confidence, as well as listening and math skills," he explained. "Studies conclude that music fosters creativity and relieves stress." He ended when Marge shouted from the front row, "Ryan, there's so much music and so little time. Let's get on with the concert."

With a broad grin, Ryan introduced Joseph to a deafening round of applause.

Scarlett watched as Joseph claimed his stool and took command of the stage. He studied the audience, his gaze drifting up and down the rows as if he were searching for someone. He looked breathtakingly handsome in his concert attire—black pants and a white dress shirt, and his broad shoulders filled out the shirt to perfection. He acknowledged Dorothy in the front row next to Marge with a tip of his head.

He played the instantly recognizable chord from his Grammy-award-nominated hit, "Sing Glory Forever." When the audience cheered, he smiled and encouraged everyone to sing along.

As she peeked from the curtain, tears blurred Scarlett's view of him. She'd listened to his songs countless times on his CD, and she loved them all.

As the one hour concert sped to its finale, Joanna whispered to Russell, "Are you nervous?" The children would go on stage for the final numbers.

When it was time, Scarlett encouraged each child with a quick hug, and sent them in single file on stage. As Joanna passed Joseph, she beckoned him to bend down and whispered something in his ear.

He looked around, expressions of hope, surprise, and happiness dancing across his handsome face.

Then he smiled at the children. "Ready?" he asked.

"'And we sing, you are our God ...'" His familiar tenor voice resonated throughout the crowd, throughout the tent, and Joanna and the others joined him on the refrain.

After his second song ended, silence reigned for a beat. Then Joseph and the children bowed to a standing ovation.

Scarlett high-fived each child as they marched offstage, congratulating them on an outstanding performance.

"I'll take you all out for ice cream." She laughed. "Or salad."

"Ice cream!" they shouted in unison.

Isaac appeared. "I got here just in time. And I'll take you up on your offer for ice cream."

"You're on." She pulled back the curtain in time to see Dorothy gesture to the audience.

"Ladies and gentlemen," Dorothy said, "let's thank Joseph Slater and the children from Big Brothers and Big Sisters once more." Amidst another standing ovation, she started for the stage, but stopped as Joseph held up a hand.

"I have one more song I'd like to sing," he said. "I've been writing it ever since I came to Cherish." He cleared his throat, seeming nervous as he thumbed his guitar strings. "She's someone I think about all the time, and I want to wish her a happy Valentine's Day. And to tell her that she's the love of my life."

He hesitated, strummed a chord. "The name of the song is, 'I Need to Learn.'"

Scarlett stepped back, her hand pressed to her mouth. Was she breathing?

At first, he sang the lyrics softly. "'I need to learn that I don't got to travel anymore. / You're small town, I'm big city / but we both look at the same sky, both love the same God. / Oh, Scarlett, Scarlett, you've taught me how to dream."

Somewhere behind her, Scarlett heard Isaac ask in a whisper, "Scarlett, should I get your coat?"

She couldn't answer. She forgot about her coat. She forgot about everything in the world around her.

When Joseph sang her name again, sang about love, she touched her hand to her heart, the tears flowing freely. Everything around her seemed to quiet.

Somehow, Dorothy's hand had linked to her arm.

"He wants you to come on stage," Dorothy said.

"How?" Scarlett asked.

"By walking with me."

On legs like rubber, she followed as Dorothy guided her. "He's been writing this song for weeks," Dorothy went on, whispering in Scarlett's ear. "At first, I asked if he wanted my help with the lyrics. He said he didn't need my help, because the lyrics just flowed. He asked me to give the song to you this evening, but then Joanna told him you were here when she went out to sing."

Now they were on stage. Scarlett stepped into the spotlight, and Dorothy moved to the side.

Joseph set down his guitar, pushed back the microphone. He stood and came to her.

Her heart took a leap. He stood straight and tall, aching tenderness in his blue eyes. Up close, he looked a bit scruffy, hardly put together, like a man who had been pacing for days. His wavy hair was tousled, as if he'd incessantly run a hand through it. And he'd skipped a button on his shirt.

Still reeling, she gazed up at him as he fingered the highlighted strands of green hair around her face. He grinned and whispered, "No blue?"

"Just green."

He took her hands in his. "'I don't got to travel anymore,'" he sang softly, "'because I'm home.'" Certainty shone in his eyes. "'And we're both going to love each other right here in Cherish.'" The softness of his breath brushed against her cheek as he bent to kiss her.

He was professing his love in front of the entire town, hundreds of people. And wasn't all this being recorded?

She swallowed. "You're flying to Raleigh tomorrow." The risk of tears had passed, the lump in her throat disappearing. A stubble covered his jaw, shadows beneath his eyes, but his gaze radiated expectation and hope.

"I canceled it."

"Joseph, you shouldn't. Not for me."

He pressed his finger to her lips. "I did it for us. I'd much rather be here with you."

The moment Scarlett stirred, Dorothy and Ryan rushed over, and Dorothy jostled Scarlett and Joseph away from the spotlight.

"Quite the encore, you two lovebirds." Dorothy's lips trembled with laughter.

"How's that for a real Valentine's Day surprise?" Ryan joked to the audience with a wry smile. "A true happily ever after." He thanked everyone as murmurings grew to a fever-pitch, then asked the technicians to play one of Joseph's songs and turn up the volume.

* * *

Two hours later, as a light gentle wind teased the air, Scarlett and Joseph walked to the inn holding hands.

"The children enjoyed their ice cream," he said.

"Originally, Joanna had wanted candy for Valentine's Day, but she was okay with ice cream after all."

"And you ordered low-fat frozen yogurt."

She smiled. "My new favorite dessert."

"And now they're safely back at Big Brothers with Isaac."

"They deserved the applause, the ice cream, everything," Scarlett said. "They were awesome."

"And I'm going to be mentoring Russell personally."

Personally. A commitment. She laid her hand against his cheek. "You're a good man."

"I try."

They settled on the inn's porch on an old-fashioned love seat, until only a sliver of moonlight lit the sky. Once again, they held hands.

"I'm going to spend the next few weeks here at the inn. The owner, Tom, okayed it," Joseph said. "I told him my booking was temporary, just until we got married."

"You and Tom?"

He laughed softly. "You and I." He brushed a strand of hair from her temple. "Will you marry me?"

The flutter in her heart went straight to her belly. "Joseph, are you sure you've thought this through? Your fans are waiting for you all across the country."

"Other excellent worship artists will cover for me. While you were sorting ice cream flavors, I made a few phone calls."

"What about Australia?"

"I guess you'll have to come with me."

"I'm not sure. I might …"

"If and when the time comes, we'll discuss it." He kissed her forehead, her nose, her cheeks.

She chuckled. "Do you need glasses?"

"I don't think so. Why?"

"Because your aim needs to improve." She lifted her lips for a kiss.

After the kiss, he held her. "In the meantime, I'm a concert artist without a concert. Guess I'll be settling in Cherish with a certain green-haired redhead."

In the flicker of moonlight, she leaned back and gazed up at him. "Are you sure you like it here?"

"I love it. I'm even planning to lead the contemporary worship service at church. That is, if they'll have me."

"Suppose all this doesn't work out? What about your wanderlust?"

"Together, we'll pray." He threaded his fingers through her hair. The curls were well beyond unmanageable by now. "God will show us the way."

"Us?"

"You and me. Husband and wife. Trust me, we can do it all."

She stared at him. "I didn't expect this."

"What *did* you expect?"

Truly, it was all a wonderful dream, with his arms securely around her.

"I assumed we would talk after the concert and hoped we would reconcile," she said.

"We did."

Absurdly happy, she laughed.

He framed her face between his fingers. "So, will you marry me?"

"Yes, yes." She nodded, nestled closer.

"I want children. I want a family." He brushed kisses on her cheeks.

"So do I." He wanted the same things she did—love and family—the things that mattered.

"I have something for you for Valentine's Day," he said.

"You wrote me a love song." She pressed her face against his broad chest, heard the solid beating of his heart. "Isn't that romantic enough?"

"Not on Valentine's Day." He stood and strode into the inn's lobby, emerging with a bouquet of hand-picked violets, a nearly illegibly written card attached to them.

She read the note aloud. "'Scarlett with two t's, you taught me that dreams can come true. Don't give up on me.'"

"I never did," she said quietly.

"Thank you." Joseph swallowed, always in tune with her, knowing the moment was poignant for both of them. "Tom's a good guy, keeping these flowers in water since I picked them this morning."

"He's the best."

Tenderly, Joseph stared at her. "Scarlett Evans, I love you. And when I didn't see you for a couple days, I realized if I left, I would have missed the most important person in my life. God brought me to Cherish for a reason."

"God's plan is perfect." She held the flowers close as Joseph's lips captured hers.

His kisses were sweet, his closeness warm and inviting. She planned to stay with him, here in Cherish, or wherever he traveled, forever.

As evening air touched her cheeks, she watched the twinkle of stars overhead, the landscape of Cherish ever changing, yet eternally the same. Like life itself. Strong, faithful, and always good.

What a perfect Valentine's Day. A wonderful sweet journey.

"I will always love you, Joseph Slater. Always." For the rest of her life when she remembered this special day, she knew she would cry tears of joy.

For God had given her a Valentine's Day to cherish.

The End

A NOTE FROM JOSIE

Thank you for reading *A Valentine To Cherish*. I hope you enjoyed your visit to the scenic town of Cherish, South Carolina, the music store, Musically Yours, and all of the wonderful characters, including Scarlett and Joseph.

If you loved this inspirational romance as much as I loved writing it, please help other people find *A Valentine To Cherish* by posting your review, as well as for the bundle: Romance Stories To Cherish.

A Valentine To Cherish is available in ebook, paperback, Large Print paperback, Hardcover, and audiobook.

If you love adorable puppies and the holidays, you'll enjoy the 4th book in the series, A Christmas Puppy To Cherish.

The 5th book is A Homecoming To Cherish, featuring a single mother struggling to raise her teenage daughter.

The final book in the series is A Summer To Cherish, featuring a despondent artist losing his vision, and the spunky, independent woman who encourages him.

I'd love to meet you in person someday, but in the meantime, all I can offer is a sincere and grateful thank you. Without your support, my books would not be possible.

As I write my next sweet or inspirational romance, remember this: Have you ever tried something you were afraid to try because it mattered so much to you? I did, when I started writing. Take the chance, and just do something you love.

My Spotify Play List for A Valentine To Cherish is here.

With sincere appreciation,

Josie Riviera

Want more sweet Valentine romances?

Check out:

I Love You More

1-800-CUPID

A Valentine To Cherish

A Chocolate-Box Valentine

Valentine Hearts: Sweet and inspirational Valentine romances!

Want more of the inspirational Cherish series?

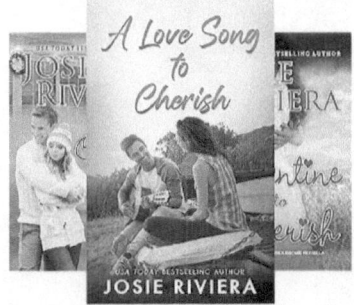

Or grab Cherished Hearts.

The entire series! 6 sweet, inspirational romances in 1 giant boxed set.

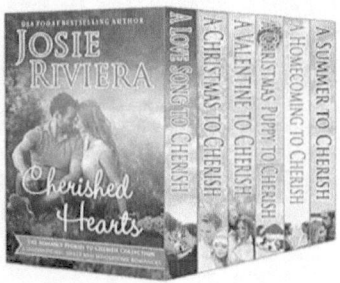

VALENTINE-SHAPED MEATLOAF RECIPE

Meatloaf (preheat oven to 350 degrees F)

2 pounds meatloaf mix (beef/pork/veal)
    1 medium onion, diced fine
    1 loaf of Italian bread or French baguette, stale
    1/4 cup of milk
    2 eggs
    1/2 cup Parmesan cheese
    1 tablespoon garlic powder
    1 teaspoon salt
    1/4 teaspoon pepper
    1 teaspoon Italian seasoning

1. Cut loaf of bread in half the night before you are going to make the meatloaf and cover it with paper towels.

2. When you are ready to start your meatloaf, remove all of the bread from the crust. Use the crust for something else.

3. Put the bread in a large bowl, and add the milk. Stir it to get the bread saturated.

4. Once the bread is saturated, squeeze out some of the milk. You want it wet, but not dripping. Pour out the excess milk and put the bread back into the large bowl. Add the onion, eggs, cheese, garlic powder, salt, pepper, and Italian seasoning. Mix well.

5. Add the meat to the bowl and with your hands mix everything thoroughly. Shape the meatloaf into a heart shape.

6. Place the meatloaf into a 1-inch deep pan.

7. Place in oven and cook for about 1 hour. Check to make sure the internal temperature is 165 degrees F.

Barbecue Sauce
    1 can tomato sauce
    1 tablespoon spicy brown mustard
    1/4 to 1/2 cup brown sugar (to taste)

1. Mix in bowl and set aside until the meatloaf has cooked for 1 hour. Carefully drain fat from the meatloaf pan. Pour barbecue sauce over meatloaf and put it back in the oven for 15 minutes. Remove from oven. Tent with foil until ready to assemble.

Mashed Potatoes:
    2 pounds russet potatoes
    4 tablespoons butter (I prefer unsalted butter)
    1/2 cup sour cream
    Salt & pepper to taste

Milk for thinning out the potatoes, as necessary

1. Peel potatoes, cut into 1-inch cubes, then rinse. Place in a 2-quart saucepan with enough water to cover the potatoes and add 1 teaspoon of salt to the water. Bring the potatoes to a boil and after 20 minutes, check them for tenderness. If not quite done, check every 2 minutes until done.
2. Drain potatoes in a colander, and put back in the pot. Put the pot back on the stove on high. Shake the pan to dry the potatoes. When dry, move the potatoes to a bowl, add the butter, and using a mixer mix the potatoes until there are no lumps. (Using a potato masher will not add air to the potatoes to make them fluffy.) Mix in the sour cream. Add milk to lighten the potatoes, but still allow them to stay in peaks when you pull the mixer out. Add salt and pepper to taste.

How to assemble:

1. Place meatloaf onto a platter with at least 3 inches of room around the meatloaf.
2. Spoon potatoes around the heart shaped meatloaf to look lacy. Using a teaspoon put little depressions in the potatoes.
3. You can pour some more of the BBQ sauce from the pan onto the meatloaf, but not a lot. Serve the BBQ sauce in a gravy boat.
4. Add a favorite vegetable and enjoy!

A CHRISTMAS PUPPY TO CHERISH CHAPTER ONE PREVIEW

CHAPTER ONE

Maxwell Archer gave up. The harmonica wasn't there.

He might as well walk the short distance from his rental home in Cherish, South Carolina, to Musically Yours, the local music store. The store was reputed to be the finest in town. Likewise, it was also the only music store in the small town.

Open suitcases lay on the floor in the compact, plain living room of his rental. Further cluttering the room was a confusion of chirping budgies, oversized birdcages, and a stack of research notes piled beside his computer. He definitely needed some air.

Momentarily diverted by Angel, a silvery green budgie who chattered, "God bless us, every one," over and over, Max shrugged on his olive-green twill jacket, uttered a brief good-bye, and headed out the door.

He'd recited numerous words to his parakeets. The key to teaching a parakeet to talk was repetition, but "God bless us, every one," was the only phrase Angel repeated. She was a rescue bird, and her previous owner had been an elderly woman who apparently had watched Charles Dickens's, *A Christmas Carol*, on television many times.

The other two parakeets—one timid, the other bolder—squawked, chirped, and carried on between themselves.

As Max strolled, a brisk December breeze invigorated him, and he paused to regard the poignantly familiar mom and pop shops. Whitney's, the ice cream store, and Big Brothers Big Sisters, where he'd spent many afternoons after school finishing his homework. The brick building looked the same.

At twelve years old, Max had delivered the *Sunday Sentinel* to all the businesses along Main Street, accompanied by a racing dog his foster family, the Monroes, had owned. He remembered that dog. He loved that dog. A Labrador husky named Tinsel.

He couldn't contain his smile as he reminisced.

The calendar showed December fifth, and downtown was in the process of being transformed into a Yuletide fairyland. Numerous workers scurried past him, draping tiny white lights on bushes and sprinkling artificial snow over minia-ture pine trees.

Through the years, he'd indulged in visions of settling here in Cherish. He had envisioned a prestigious house on the prosperous outskirts and living out his days wealthy and respected.

Three decades had passed, and he hadn't accumulated wealth in any sense of the word. In fact, his last year's research project had been stalled because of insufficient funding.

And respected? In academic circles, perhaps. He fingered the bow tie beneath his chin—his acknowledgement to the realm of academic nerds, in which he was a charter member.

In any event, his appointment to the ornithology depart-ment of a large university in Jacksonville, Florida, began January first.

As he stepped inside the music store, a slim woman with dark hair and striking green eyes greeted him.

"May I help you?" she asked.

He nodded toward the frosted-glass front window deco-rated with treble clef signs, animated polar bears, and a model train weaving around an ice-covered mountain scene. "Nice." He made a comical face. "The motifs enhance the window with a …"

She raised an eyebrow. "Festive touch?"

"Complete with tiny icicles." He moved inside, toward a shelf crammed with key holders and picked up a key holder shaped like an amplifier. Clever. However, he doubted he was allowed to hammer nails into his temporary rental house.

He sighed and surveyed the tidy store. "Do you sell harmonicas?" he asked.

"Yes. A wide assortment." The woman nodded toward a side wall. "Is this for a Christmas gift?"

"For myself. I lost my harmonica during my move." He rubbed his shoulders and unzipped his jacket. Though his rental was furnished, his limbs ached from lifting heavy bird cages and suitcases. He was an academic, not a body-builder.

In addition, his brain was flooded with information. He'd been embedded in research the entire morning when he should have been unpacking. The hours flew by whenever he examined data and he frequently lost track of time.

"Any particular brand or style?" she was asking.

"Fenders. Key of C."

"I'll show you our bestseller, which comes with a vented plastic case." She wended around numerous aisles, located a gold-edged case on a display shelf, and handed it to him. "Here's our most popular model. A twenty-tone diatonic harmonica in the key of C."

"An exact replacement for the one I lost." He ran his fingers along the case. "Thanks."

A sudden, booming symphony burst through the speakers, and they both jumped.

"Sorry," the woman said. "The background music in the store constantly needs adjustment." With a self-conscious grin, she dashed to the counter and lowered the volume. "Beethoven will do that."

"Do what?

"Startle customers with crashing chords." She darted him a sideways glance. "I haven't seen you before, by the way."

Well, that didn't take long, he thought. A stranger in a small town called for questions from the local shop owner.

"I lived here for a brief spell when I attended junior high school," he said. "I arrived yesterday after an almost three-decade absence."

She didn't press for additional information, and he didn't elaborate.

"Are you here permanently?" she asked.

"Only for December. Then I'm off to my dream job in Florida." Again, he massaged his nape. Was it from the move or stress? "My name is Max, by the way. Maxwell Archer."

"Hi, Max. I'm Dorothy Edwards. My husband, Ryan, and I own this store and we sell music, instruments, and fun novelties. We also offer lessons if you're ever interested."

"Which instruments?"

"Harp, voice, guitar and piano." She hailed an entering customer with a warm smile. "Joanna, are you here for your harp lesson with Ms. Emmanuelle?"

The little girl nodded.

"She's waiting in her studio."

"Thanks. Is the puppy here? Ms. Emmanuelle mentioned that he might be."

"He's in the back."

"Yay!" The girl's face brightened. "Sorry, I'm late." She clutched her music to her chest and hurried past them.

"Joanna attends Big Brothers Big Sisters," Dorothy said. "Are you familiar with the organization?"

"Yes."

Uncertain where the conversation might be leading, Max looked away. The last subject he cared to discuss was the Big Brothers program. He remembered it well. Fond memories surfaced. Some not so fond as well, but those weren't because of the excellent program.

"Scarlett, who is married to Joseph Slater, is heavily involved," Dorothy went on. "Emmanuelle is providing Joanna with free instruction and a harp. Joseph is a well-known worship singer and songwriter. He's also on our staff when he isn't touring."

"I've never heard of him," Max said.

"Do you listen to contemporary Christian music?"

"Never." Max dismissed her inquiry with a wave. "Does

119

anyone teach harmonica? I play for fun, not professionally, but always appreciate any tips."

"Sorry, we don't. Try YouTube," she joked.

He had. He did. On a shoe-string academic budget, self-taught lessons suited Max perfectly. Learning had little to do with musicality, and more to do with determination, goal-setting, and an appreciation for music.

Dorothy set the harmonica on the counter. "What brings you here, Max?"

"I study budgies and how they mimic birdsongs and music." He smiled and handed her his credit card.

She rang up the order. "The two are related?"

"Absolutely. To quote a noted philosopher, 'birds vocalize conventional scales.'"

"Interesting."

Interesting? The fact was more than interesting.

"You studied birds in college?" she asked.

"Yes. I earned a master's degree from a New York City university affiliated with the Audubon Society."

"Is New York City home for you?"

"I don't have a permanent home. I drove down from New York to Cherish yesterday."

"A ten-hour trip," she commiserated. "My husband travels to Atlanta for opera rehearsals, and the four hours back and forth is exhausting."

"My trip was quite an adventure—to put it mildly, especially with three parakeets, all my possessions stuffed into two suitcases and a canvas backpack." He grimaced as he recalled the harrowing journey through the icy Virginia mountains.

"The birds stayed in their cages?"

"I can't imagine them flying around my van while I drive. I secured their cages with seat belts." Max leaned forward, warming to the conversation. "For safety reasons, I always remove the mirrors, bells, and swings, and placed their wooden perches close to the bottom of their cages. And I keep bottled water handy for refilling their cups."

"Good to know." Dorothy shot him a tongue-in-cheek smile. "Not that I ever plan on purchasing a pet. My brother, Nicholas, owns Molly Belle, an overgrown pup who gets into everything. That dog cured me of owning any animals."

Max chuckled. "In some respects, birds are easier than dogs."

"Nicholas is trying to find a home for a puppy that showed up at the sheriff's station a couple days ago. Are you interested?"

"What type of dog?"

"He's guessing a mixed breed—a toy poodle and Yorkshire Terrier."

"A Yorkipoo."

"Maybe. He's a real cutie, brown with silvery-white markings." She paused. "Wait. I'll be right back."

Dorothy emerged two minutes later clasping a puppy to her chest. She set him down and the puppy bound forward in little jumps, then stuck his nose under the counter. Furiously, he tugged on a pencil that had fallen.

"No, no. He loves to chew." At the sound of Dorothy's voice, the little ball of fur rushed headlong down an aisle, apparently unheeding of her calls. He turned a corner and almost lost his balance. Dorothy scooped him up and brought him over to Max. He licked Max's outstretched fingers as he petted him.

"He's a cute pup, isn't he?" Dorothy asked.

"He's also a bundle of charming, unrestrained energy."

"Any chance—"

"Sorry." Max shook his head. "I'm only in town for a month." Plus, he'd vowed never to own a dog again. He'd missed Tinsel too much after he'd been placed with another foster family.

Dorothy returned the puppy to the back room, then placed Max's harmonica and a complimentary candy cane in a bag. "I'm sorry it's such a short stay, but this town is welcoming, especially during the Christmas season."

Max expected he'd enjoy spending December in Cherish. The lease on his apartment in New York had ended, and he'd preferred to travel in early December rather than January.

"Are you a musician?" she asked, offering an irrepressible grin. "Naturally you are—considering you're in a music store purchasing a harmonica. Ryan and I are—"

"Concert artists."

She handed the bag to him. "I'm a pianist."

"And Ryan is an opera singer."

She tipped her head. "How did you know?"

"My friend Gerry Adams lives in Perrytown. He often shops in your store."

Unlike many of the undergraduate students Max taught his online Joy of Birdwatching classes to, Gerry had been interested and engaged. Most of Max's students selected his course as an easy elective.

Not Gerry. In his fifties, he'd developed an increasing appreciation for Max's expertise that had led to a friendly rapport between the two men. Gerry had become a sort of guru, offering guidance and awareness on another subject that interested Max: music.

"I know him." A smile dawned on Dorothy's face. "Gerry sings in the choir at Memorial Street Church."

No comment on the church part, though Max had recognized the wooden sign mounted above the store's entrance.

Proverbs 19:21.

He once knew the proverb, but could no longer recall the words.

Dorothy cast her gaze heavenward. "'Many are the plans in a person's heart, but it is the Lord's purpose that prevails,'" she recited.

Max kept silent.

Memories of sitting in a stiff pew during Sunday services came back in a blink. He'd tried, but he'd never pleased God as a child. He never pleased God as an adult, either. Where was the path to peace God promised? It remained elusive.

The successes Max had achieved hadn't been enough. Thus, at the age of twenty-five, he'd given up on religion.

As far as his career, he sometimes wondered if he was on the right path. Was his research nothing more than a "fluffy" elective for uninterested college freshmen? Society seemed to think along those lines, and reports through the academic grapevine whispered that ornithology programs were soon to be scrapped.

Sure, Max was appreciated—which was the reason why he was in hamster-wheel performance mode—to continue proving himself to his colleagues.

"Gerry and I are in a band," he replied, when he realized Dorothy waited for him to say something. "We rehearse online."

"Online?" Her brow furrowed.

"You're a professional, so you expect frequent in-person rehearsals. But our band rehearses virtually every week. Technology is marvelous, isn't it?"

"Not as rewarding as live rehearsals, though."

Max had to agree. "There's a likelihood Gerry and I will perform this month, if we can find a venue."

"Inquire at The Garden Terrace restaurant. The owners book entertainment on Friday evenings. In addition, I'd be delighted to host you here at the store. Do you have any CDs for sale?"

"You're kidding, right?"

"What's the name of your band?"

"The Bearded Elves."

"Hmm. Neither of you sports a beard."

"We change our name with the season."

She grinned. "When February hits, you'll become …"

"The Bearded Valentines. But I won't be here in February. My work takes me all over the US, and I'm headed to Florida in January."

"Well, I look forward to hearing you perform this month."

"Thanks. Gerry encouraged me to rent a place in Cherish. He believes all this down-home goodness is beneficial for me."

"You're on a vacation the entire month?"

"I'm rarely on vacation."

"No wife or children?" Pointedly, she peered at his left hand.

"Neither. You're looking at a forty-year-old bachelor."

She granted a conspiratorial smile. "The right woman will come along and change your mind."

"I doubt it. Women can be … exasperating."

She chuckled. "Will you travel to New York for Christmas?"

"I'll spend Christmas day with Gerry, his wife, Melissa, and their newborn colicky son. They're first-time parents."

Dorothy rolled her eyes. "So I've heard."

Besides Gerry, there was no one else, Max thought. Unless Max's foster brother, John, who resided in a faraway Portuguese village, counted.

It didn't matter. The season had lost its meaning eons ago. December twenty-fifth was just another day that passed in the flicker of an eye.

Dorothy's fixed smile didn't vacillate. She seemed the sort who put immense emphasis on the holidays.

He shifted. "I'm grateful for the opportunity to hunker down with my research this month."

At Dorothy's quizzical glance, he added, "On birds."

"Along with performing a live gig or two."

"Gerry and I aren't expert musicians like you and your husband, or that Slater worship singer guy. Our specialty is performing at roadside diners for a free meal."

"I well remember those days." She shook her head. "Since you'll be working here for the month, do you need any assistance with your research?"

"Can you recommend someone who could go birding with me tomorrow morning? I'd appreciate a guide."

Dorothy studied him. "I picture you in a forest, some-where more suited to your rugged looks, rather than writing papers. You must spend a great deal of time outdoors."

"I try." He pushed a hand through his thick hair. When had he last gotten it cut? "The Carolinas have various bird species I'd like to listen to."

"Your parakeets will truly mimic other birds?"

"Optimistically, although I haven't had much luck with them imitating anything."

Except "God bless us, every one."

"I know the ideal woman," Dorothy said.

"She likes nature?"

"Absolutely, and she's passionate about hiking." A gleam of mischief shone in Dorothy's eyes. "She works at Thumbs Up, a local florist, but might be off tomorrow. I'll text her."

"What's her name?"

"Sarah Hartman." Dorothy snatched a cell phone from beneath the counter. "She dropped out of college to care for her elderly aunt, then went on to pursue a degree in floral design."

"How old is she?"

"Sarah turned thirty last month. She's the type who

juggles a half dozen projects, numerous details, and never gets frustrated. And ..." Dorothy paused to accentuate the words. "Her flower arrangements are exquisite."

He'd never purchased store-bought flowers in his life. The most magnificent blossoms—miniature red roses, deep violets, and pale blue ivy—spilled alongside brooks or grew wild in a field.

A response flew across Dorothy's phone screen. "Sarah confirmed she's not working until tomorrow afternoon," Dorothy read. "She had plans but is happy to change them. What's your address, Max?"

"I rented a house a couple blocks from here. It's 8 Poplar Lane. Tell her I'll bring the hiking essentials."

Dorothy typed into her phone, then delivered the response. "She'll pick you up in the morning."

"A hiker and a florist is an attractive combination."

"Oh, and she's plenty more. Animals love her. The cat at the greenhouse that handles mice won't let anyone near her except Sarah. Likewise, dogs practically grovel at her feet." Dorothy glanced up. "Remember Molly Belle?"

"Your brother's unruly dog?"

Dorothy choked a giggle. "She adores everyone and is beyond energetic, although remarkably calm and obedient around Sarah."

"Does Sarah own any pets?"

"Are you giving away birds?"

"I'd never part with my parakeets. Angel is the oldest, and she's been with me for several years." He lifted a quizzical brow. "What about Sarah?"

"She owns a few animals."

"Is she married?" He didn't want an irate husband or boyfriend on his tail for going birdwatching with Sarah.

"She's coming off a sorry relationship, but you'll discover she's a stunner."

Another word for mantrap. He understood the type well after dating a flirtatious woman who'd been beautiful enough to be on the cover of *Vogue* but who abruptly ended their month of dating with a cursory text.

From that point forward, he'd avoided any romantic overtures from beautiful women. They were interested in a guy's money and power. As soon as they realized Max had neither, they hightailed it out of his life.

"You'll learn all about her tomorrow." Dorothy peered at the phone screen, grinned, then snapped it shut. "She drives a yellow pickup truck and said she'll see you at eight."

*** End of Excerpt *A Christmas Puppy to Cherish* by Josie Riviera ***

Copyright © 2020 Josie Riviera

Keep reading on Amazon. FREE on Kindle Unlimited.

ABOUT THE AUTHOR

Josie Riviera is a USA TODAY bestselling author of contemporary, inspirational, and historical sweet romances that read like Hallmark movies. She lives in the Charlotte, NC, area with her wonderfully supportive husband. They share their home with an adorable shih tzu, who constantly needs grooming, and live in an old house forever needing renovations.

To receive my Newsletter and your free sweet romance novella ebook as a thank you gift, sign up <u>HERE.</u>

Become a member of my Read and Review VIP Facebook group for exclusive giveaways and ARCs.

josieriviera.com

ACKNOWLEDGMENTS

To my patient husband, Dave, and our three wonderful children.

ALSO BY JOSIE RIVIERA

Seeking Patience

Seeking Catherine (always Free!)

Seeking Fortune

Seeking Charity

Seeking Rachel

The Seeking Series

Oh Danny Boy

I Love You More

A Snowy White Christmas

A Portuguese Christmas

Holiday Hearts Book Bundle Volume One

Holiday Hearts Book Bundle Volume Two

Holiday Hearts Book Bundle Volume Three

Holiday Hearts Book Bundle Volume Four

Holiday Hearts Book Bundle Volume Five

Candleglow and Mistletoe

Maeve (Perfect Match)

A Christmas To Cherish

A Love Song To Cherish

A Valentine To Cherish

A Christmas Puppy To Cherish

A Homecoming To Cherish

Romance Stories To Cherish

Aloha to Love

Sweet Peppermint Kisses

Valentine Hearts Boxed Set

1-800-CUPID

1-800-CHRISTMAS

1-800-IRELAND

1-800-SUMMER

1-800-NEW YEAR

The 1-800-Series Sweet Contemporary Romance Bundle

Irish Hearts Sweet Romance Bundle

Holly's Gift

A Chocolate-Box Valentine

A Chocolate-Box Christmas

A Chocolate-Box New Years

A Chocolate-Box Summer Breeze

A Chocolate-Box Christmas Wish

A Chocolate-Box Irish Wedding

Chocolate-Box Hearts

Chocolate-Box Hearts Volume Two

Chocolate-Box Double Hearts

Recipes from the Heart

Leading Hearts

New Year Hearts

SENIOR HEARTS

A Summer To Cherish

Summer Hearts

Romance Stories To Cherish Volume Two

Cherished Hearts

Christmas in the Air

A Very Christian Christmas

The 1-800-Series Volume Two

The 1-800-Series Complete

Christmas Tails of the Heart

Cocoa's Christmas Love

Pawfect Christmas Hearts

Pink Coral Island

Most books are available in ebook, audiobook, paperback, Large Print paperback and Hardcover.

Many are FREE on Kindle Unlimited!

www.ingramcontent.com/pod-product-compliance
Lightning Source LLC
Chambersburg PA
CBHW030917260626
47169CB00011B/1260